THE
WARDEN'S
WIFE

by

Felicity McQuade

DORRANCE
PUBLISHING CO
EST. 1920
PITTSBURGH, PENNSYLVANIA 15235

Dorrance Publishing Co
585 Alpha Drive
Suite 103
Pittsburgh, PA 15238
Visit our website at *www.dorrancebookstore.com*

ISBN: 978-1-4809-3742-0
eISBN: 978-1-4809-3765-9

CHAPTER 1

"Are you still planning to go up to the lodge in this weather?" Melissa asked worriedly as the wind tore her words away. She was a sturdy woman, shorter than Maggie's five-feet, three-inch stature with short salt-and-pepper hair. Her usually cheerful demeanor was absent as she eyed the weather.

Maggie nodded. "Yeah, I only have this week off before the film crew gets here—I want to make sure the cabin is ready for the winter. I didn't have much time to get up there this summer to do any work."

Maggie walked out the emergency wing entrance of West Park General Hospital with her friend, Melissa, grimacing as the snow continued to whip around her. Although she hoped it wouldn't last long, the weather reports predicted eight to twelve inches before morning in the city. She knew more was accumulating at the lodge and was seriously rethinking the wisdom of driving there tonight.

"I really just want to go home and relax by the fire, but that's not going to happen. This snowstorm in the middle of October makes it even more important that I check on the cabin."

Melissa nodded and would have said more, but some of the other nurses caught up with them and invited the two friends to join the group for a quick drink before heading home.

Maggie cited her trip to the lodge as they reached the garage entrance. "I'd love to join you but I really need to get on the road. You have a good time and be safe going home, don't drink too much!"

"Don't worry, we won't promise to be good but we will be careful! I'll have a drink for you!" Melissa called after her as Maggie called her goodbyes and trekked through the slush toward her truck, which seemed to wait patiently on the snow-covered roof level of the busy hospital garage.

The wind bit harshly and Maggie pulled the scarf closer around her neck while she climbed into the usually shiny black Ford F150 4X4 truck, now covered with at least two inches of snow and started the engine turning the heat on full blast before she got out to scrape the windows and headlights. She wanted to get going before the storm got too far ahead of her. She pulled into the street and headed to Dog Day Afternoon, the doggie day care to pick up Taser, her German Shepard. She didn't usually leave him there, but it was closer to the interstate from the hospital, and Maggie had wanted to get on the highway as soon as her shift ended.

Once back in the now-warmed cab, Maggie turned on the radio and plugged in her iPod. After she scanned the playlists, she selected Muse and began to sing along with "Supermassive Black Hole" as she pulled into Dog Day Afternoon's parking lot. The pavement was icy as she gingerly walked across the lot into the single-story building. As she pulled the steel door open, the welcoming sounds of excited yipping greeted her along with the faint smell of disinfectant and dog food.

The grandmotherly woman sitting behind the reception desk widow with "Mrs. Graham" printed in black script smiled up at Maggie. Maggie returned the woman's smile. "I'm here to pick up Taser. I hope he behaved himself, he's not used to being away from home all day."

Mrs. Graham stood and shook her head. "He's very well behaved for not spending time with other dogs. Other than trying to mark everything with his scent, he was not at all aggressive toward them."

Maggie laughed. "He socializes at the field where we walk every morning so he is used to being around dogs. I try to keep him from being aggressive with other dogs though; it's no fun walking with him if he won't behave."

"That's true, it should be fun walking with them but not if they try to attack everyone and everything that comes close. He is a well-trained dog; you did a good job with him. He is welcome here anytime," Mrs. Graham stated as she presented the bill to Maggie.

Maggie swiped her debit card through the machine to pay for the day and Mrs. Graham opened the door to wave Maggie into the play area.

"Come on back and get him."

Taser came bounding over and sat looking up at Maggie, sweeping the floor with his tail in his excitement to see her. Maggie bent down and rubbed his ears snapping the leash onto his collar. Taser walked beside her to the truck and sat, waiting for her to open the back door. He jumped in and sprawled full-length over the back seat and sighing, closed his eyes.

Taser's paws made soft scratching noises on the leather upholstery while sleep running. Maggie shook her head at him. "Silly dog," she said, chuckling.

"Neutron Star Collision" came on and she sang along with Muse making good time until she got off the main highway at the crossroads to the lodge. Here, the storm continued with an unrelenting ferocity; limiting visibility to the edge of the hood. With the snow swirling around and the wind howling and buffeting the truck it began to slightly sway along the unsheltered road. She engaged the four-wheel drive and kept moving. The snow was deep making it a little easier to drive as the ice on the road was well covered. The already dim light was fading, the road barely visible even with the illumination of the headlights and fog lamps. Driving slowly, Maggie had no difficulty staying on the road listening to the gentle roar of the rumble strips under her tires along the right side of the road.

About one-third the way up the mountainous road, Maggie realized that she'd been following partially covered tire tracks. At one point, the tracks seemed to have churned up the snow as if the vehicle had been stuck. There were footprints there as well, with two sets making the snow spew about as if they had pushed the vehicle to get it moving again and a third set disappearing into the woods. She didn't pay much attention to them since she was looking for the turnoff a few hundred yards farther on. The tire tracks continued up the road when she reached the left turn that led to the lodge.

The driveway entrance was easy to miss, and Maggie was afraid she had missed it with the piling snow, but no, there it was. Maggie kept the truck in four-wheel drive as she navigated up the mile-long, snow-covered graveled track to the lodge. She was concentrating on staying on the narrow road when Taser interrupted her concentration by barking and pacing back and forth on the seat.

"Taser, down! What's gotten into you?"

Taser kept up the barking and pacing, adding a high-pitched howl while butting her with his cold, wet nose. He began to paw at the door as if he could open it and get out. Maggie slowed down and stopped the truck so she could look around at Taser and try to calm him.

She opened her door and the big German Shepard jumped over the seat and shot out of the truck.

"Taser, here!"

Maggie stumbled after him, still calling for him to come back. His raucous barks were farther away and she was beginning to get nervous by his behavior. The skin along her neck prickled, something had to be wrong because Taser always listened to her. He'd never take off like this under normal circumstances. Finally, about fifty yards from the truck, she saw Taser trotting back and then turning away for her to follow.

"What is it, Taser?"

She kept following until she saw what had disturbed him. He was pawing at a dark and bulky shadow in the snow. As Maggie moved closer, she realized that some of the darkness was blood. She bent over the shape and scrutinized the blood oozing from a deep gash in the unconscious man's head.

Maggie knelt in the snow and checked his pulse. Weak but palpable; okay that was good. What other injuries did he have? She quickly ran her hands over his neck and down his body to feel for any broken bones. As she moved her fingers over his sides, she heard a slight grating sound. It felt as if she had stuck her hand into a bowl of puffed rice and she feared he had broken ribs. She was loathe to move him, not knowing what kind of injury was under the blood running down the pale face. Maggie sat back on her heels thinking about the best course of action to take.

Maggie tried to wake him up but was unsuccessful; she made up her mind. He would have to be moved to the lodge for his injuries to be better assessed. She stumbled as she ran back through the knee-deep snow to the road and fished out the tarp and rope from the storage chest in the truck bed. With the items secured, she loped back toward the man. Taser was standing protectively over him, pawing at the bloody snow. She put the tarp on the ground and rolled the injured man onto it. After she secured it tightly around him so he wouldn't slip out, she dragged the inert form back to the truck. By the time Maggie got the man to the truck, sweat was running down her back and between her breasts, despite the cold. It was a struggle getting him inside without causing more damage, but finally she inched his lifeless form and the tarp onto the back seat and pulled from the driver's side to settle him on the bench seat. Once she had the seatbelt fastened around his waist, Maggie started the Ford and continued up the drive to the lodge.

The only movement Maggie saw from rearview mirror was the slow rise and fall of his chest. He didn't seem to have difficulty breathing and that made her feel better considering the broken ribs and the bouncing she caused when she dragged him, roughly, to the truck. She thought she hit what seemed to be every rut in the road. She had no idea how she was going to get him up the steps to the porch and in the front door. Every muscle screamed with fatigue and pain, unused to the demand she made on them this afternoon; she honestly didn't think she had the energy to move his dead weight again.

Maggie trudged slowly up the steps to the front door. The overhang had protected it from the worst of the drifts, but the snow was still deep, covering the steps that led up to the wraparound porch. She opened the door and went into the small entryway. As expected, the storm had knocked out the electricity so there was no light or heat. She shuffled into the living room hardly able to lift her feet, and put a match to the kindling waiting in the double-sided fireplace. She lingered until it caught, adding larger logs to warm the rooms, then went back outside to get the supplies out of the truck.

Maggie looked into the back seat, but the man was still unconscious. She knew she would have to get those wet clothes off of him after she figured out a way to get him into the house. After two trips she got the supplies and her clothes into the house, and made sure Taser was busy eating so he wouldn't get in her way, Maggie shoveled all the snow to one side of the steps and packed it down firmly. Once she made a sort of incline there, she went back to the truck and pulled the man out of the back seat bracing the weight of his body against her legs to prevent him from dropping into the snow. Once his feet were on the ground she lowered the tarp and began to drag the still-unconscious man up the snow ramp. It was distressingly slow because she had to pull the tarp up at an angle since she was on the steps and he was on the snow-packed ramp. Finally, after what felt like climbing Everest, she dragged the injured man into the living room deposited him in front of the now-blazing fire.

Maggie collapsed on the old sofa to catch her breath while she took off her jacket and boots. She sat there for a few more minutes thinking about what to do next. The sweaty and snow-dampened clothes were making her uncomfortable so she went into the bedroom. She really wanted nothing more than to take a hot shower, but that would have to wait; instead she dug dry clothes out of her bag and quickly changed. On her way back to the living room, she cranked the generator, grateful to hear the roar of the motor. Walking toward the inert form on the floor by the fire, Maggie began to remove his wet clothing. She tried to be gentle removing the pullover sweater because of his broken ribs and struggled for a few minutes mumbling to herself that she should just cut the damned thing off and be done with it. Removing clothing from unconscious patients in the emergency department was her least favorite job but at least there she had assistance in turning and holding patients steady while the clothing was removed. Here she was by herself and was afraid she was doing more damage to the unconscious man than helping. Her struggles were rewarded when the sweater came off over his head suddenly, nearly toppling her into the fireplace.

"Oomph! Well, I hope the rest of your clothes aren't as hard to get off you. I don't want this to take all night," Maggie mumbled to herself.

Her next task was to clean and dress his wounds. She hoped he would stay unconscious long enough to get him dry and attend to the gash in his head. She cleaned the head wound and found it wasn't as deep as she feared. There was something familiar about him once the blood was gone and she saw his face clearly. She knew him from somewhere. Where had she seen him before? She examined him for any injuries she may have missed in the snow and tried to keep her mind in professional mode. He was lean and toned, not an ounce of flab on his body. He seemed to be fit, which was a good thing; he would heal faster if he was in good shape. His hair was a soft brown, and when she opened his eyelids to examine the pupils she found his eyes were a deep blue. It wasn't a pretty face, but rather handsome and masculine, appealing with a square jaw and a nose that looked like it might have been broken at least once if the slight bump over the bridge was any indication. She found herself staring at him instead of getting on with the task at hand. She gave herself a shake and told herself to get on with the job.

After getting surgical tape and bandages from the first-aid box she kept on the built-in shelves in the short hall leading to the bath and bedroom, she applied a thin coat of antibiotic ointment to the wound. She pushed the edges of the head wound together while applying butterfly adhesive bandages to keep the edges together. When she finished, she pulled an old flannel shirt onto his body and buttoned it around his chest. As she completed this task, the man moaned and stirred, but didn't wake.

He really was good looking, even with the bruises peppering his face. She tried to remain professional, but all her good intentions melted like the snow pooling around the pile of discarded clothing when her hand bumped across his groin as she pulled the dry sweatpants up over his hips and he grew hard. She took a shaky breath and pulled her hands away; he was covered up enough for now, she decided. Still, she couldn't help the thoughts that floated through her head. She wondered what it would feel like to make love to him. She could feel heat and moisture continue to build up at the apex of her thighs. Her eyes closed as she let out a soft moan only to be startled open when a cold, wet nose inveigled its way under her arm. Taser, responding to her moan, shattered her daydream before it could get X-rated. She wrapped the man in the comforter, gave herself another shake, and decided she needed a shower—maybe a cold one.

Twenty minutes later and feeling like a new woman after a hot shower, Maggie made a cup of hot chocolate with marshmallow cream and savored every sip. Taser, curled up in front of the fire, was again running in his sleep. Maggie checked that the man's pupils reacted to the light. She again tried to wake him without success. He seemed warmer now, his breathing still regular and even, and his pulse was stronger. She got the pillows and comforters from the bed, crawled onto the floor beside him, and set the alarm for one hour.

CHAPTER 2

The alarm wakened Maggie with a start, and for a moment, she wondered why she had set the alarm at the lodge. Then she remembered and looked to her right. The man was still unmoving, but his color seemed better and his breathing was steady. She checked his pupils again with no change.

"I wish you would wake up. The longer you're out the worse your injuries could be...," she mumbled to herself. Maggie pulled the comforter around him again, reset the alarm for another hour, and drifted off to sleep.

She awoke to soft kisses along her jaw and neck. When she rolled over, he was leaning over her, his blue eyes gleaming and gold streaks formed in his hair from the fire. She reached her arm up and wrapped it around his neck. A current of awareness jolted through her system coalescing in her groin as his lips touched her again, using his tongue along the seam of her lips seeking entrance to her mouth. She welcomed the taste of him, groaning softly as his teeth nibbled on her bottom lip. Maggie felt her core clench with need. She could feel her insides tighten and moaned again, louder this time. He pushed her downward as Maggie arched upward trying to get closer to him. Their kiss deepened as he moved his hands under her sweatshirt, inching it up to uncover her breasts. He broke off the kiss only to replace his lips around her nipples. As he suckled her, his hand moved to the waistband of her sweats. She spread her legs apart, lifting her hips making it easier for him to slide the sweatpants off her and gain access. His fingers trailed heat along her center until he finally stopped and played with the bundle of nerves at her core. She bucked upward trying to make him enter her; she could feel him moan against her breast, the vibrations making the sucking sensations all the more intense. His fingers delved farther until he was at her entrance. She swore she heard bells chiming as the kiss deepened and he started to rub against her most sensitive area.

The chiming became louder and she startled awake to the sound of the alarm. It had all been a dream, it wasn't real; Maggie wanted to scream in frustration, the dream had been so intense. She could still feel her body pulsating from the desire the dream had stirred in her.

Get a grip. What is wrong with me? I need to get laid, she thought as she sat up to look at the object of her vivid dream.

This time when Maggie tried to wake the man, he moaned and moved. She kept talking to him, again thinking he looked familiar. After a few minutes, he opened his eyes and looked around the room.

"Where am I?" His voice was weak and hoarse.

Maggie got a glass of water from the nearby table and put it to his lips to help him swallow.

"You're at my great-great-grandfather's lodge. I found you—or, rather, Taser did, in the woods. You were wet and hurt so I brought you here. What's your name?"

Maggie sat on the floor next to him. He looked around the room and then focused on Maggie.

"What happened to me?" He started to sit up and, turning pale, lay back groaning.

"We're about forty-five miles northeast of Pittsburgh. Just lie back. You've probably got a concussion, judging by the gash in your head. Taser found you, unconscious in the woods and led me to you. You're kinda banged up, looks like you went a round or two with Mike Tyson. You have bruises everywhere. Your ribs are broken, so don't move around too much, I can't do anything if you puncture a lung. You were pretty cold and wet when we got here; your clothes are drying by the chimney in the other room. It's early Saturday morning, around three. I found you around six-thirty last night. Do you remember anything?"

He started to shake his head but stopped with a groan. "Not a thing. My clothes are drying by the fire? You undressed me? Took care of me?" His eyes traveled her length and started to shake his head again, but thought better of it. "How?"

"I'm a nurse; I learned how to do those things. It looks like you took quite a beating. I'm Maggie Jones. What's your name?"

"I'm...." He looked at Maggie in somewhat of a panic.

Maggie tried to reassure him by telling him that it wasn't unusual to have some memory loss after a concussion. "I believe after some rest your memory will come back to you. Does your head hurt?"

"Just a sort of dull ache. Could I have some more water?"

Maggie helped him sit up and gave him more water and two acetaminophen tablets cautioning him to sip slowly. Once again, she had a sense of déjà vu when she looked at him, thinking she knew him. She helped him back down onto the pillow. "I'm sorry about you lying on the floor; I couldn't get you onto the bed, you're a little too big for me to lift from the floor and I was just too tired to try. Besides, I thought it would be warmer if I kept you closer to the fire. I can try to help you get to the bed now if you like."

"Not necessary, I think I'll stay put for now, I'm not sure I can move. My head is pounding and I'm a little dizzy. Have you been here beside me all night?" he asked as he saw the second comforter and pillows by the fire.

"Yes, I wanted to keep an eye on you, I've been checking on you every hour."

The deep timbre of his voice washed over her and suddenly she knew who he was.

"Oh. My. God. I do know you! It's been driving me crazy that I thought I knew you and for the life of me couldn't figure out how. You're Tyler Sinclair. You're an actor, making a movie in Pittsburgh."

"That's my name, Tyler Sinclair?" His voice made the sentence a question as his brow furrowed.

"I'm sure that's who you are. I hadn't heard that you were in town yet though. In the morning, my cell phone should be charged so I can call for help; get you to the hospital. In the meantime, you look pretty wiped out. Why don't you try to get some more sleep?"

Maggie stoked the fire and added a few logs to keep the place warm. She turned and found Tyler watching her.

"The storm knocked out the power lines coming from the main road. The generator is to keep the pipes from freezing since I turned the water back on and for light. There is no central heat so the fireplace is the only heat we have. The storm's going to get worse over the next few hours. Once it gets light and the road crews start up the mountain, I'll give them a call to let them know I'm up here so they can clear the bottom of the drive. Then I'll get you to the hospital."

Maggie made sure that Tyler was as comfortable as he could be on the floor. She got back under her comforter and tried to sleep. Outside, the storm raged on, lightning illuminated the sky, and the thunder rolled. She hated thunderstorms in the winter. For some reason they scared her more than the ones in summer. Besides, the man lying next to her disturbed her, or rather he unsettled her. She listened to his breathing as he slept and turned over so she could watch the flames for a while hoping they would make her sleepy; eventually, she fell into a deep sleep.

CHAPTER 3

Both Maggie and Tyler started out of a deep sleep when a loud clap of thunder shook the lodge. Another flash of lightning split the night, and the front of the lodge lit up, followed by an ear-splitting crash. Maggie jumped up and ran to the door.

"NO!" she cried when she opened the door and stepped out to the destruction in front of her. She sagged against the doorframe and clung to the worn wood for support.

"Maggie, what is it? What's wrong?" Tyler sat up and attempted to stand, holding on to the worn sofa.

Her voice was strained and filled with tears as she turned to answer him. "Lightning hit one of the trees and toppled it; it fell on my truck, crushing it completely. Part of the porch was hit as well, and the roof collapsed over the truck bed." As she continued to explain what had happened, her voice shifted to nurse report mode to try to stave off the fear and anxiety she felt at the realization that they were stranded here. "At least it's the side opposite the woodpile. I'm afraid we're going to be stuck here for a while." Maggie turned to him, her face a pale shape in the dim light of the fire. She looked worried and defeated as she sank to the floor.

"How long a while, Maggie?"

"At least until I can get inside the truck to get my phone. Otherwise, I'm not expected back at work until next Sunday. I'm sorry." Maggie felt ready to cry. She was still afraid that Tyler might be more seriously hurt than she could detect even if he seemed fine now. Another thought popped into her head and she worried that the tire tracks she had seen earlier meant that those third set of footprints belonged to Tyler. Maybe the people in the car were looking for him too.

"All right, then we're stuck here. Was does that mean? Will we be okay?"

"I stopped for supplies on my way here. There's plenty of wood for the fire. I've lots of bottled water and canned food: soups and stews and such. Camping food that doesn't need refrigerated. I was planning to stay for a few days to get the place ready for winter. I'm worried about you, though. You could be hurt more seriously than I can determine. You'll need to tell me immediately if you start having difficulty seeing or breathing or if your head hurts more than it does now."

"If it will ease your mind, I will tell you immediately if any of these things happen." Tyler grinned at her and winked.

Maggie could see that he wasn't taking her warnings too seriously and she opened her mouth to berate him when Tyler spoke again.

"You said before that I'm here to make a movie? Do you know what it's about?"

Maggie saw through his attempt to change the subject but let it go. As long as he was able to string words together to form a sentence she figured he was okay.

"You're making a movie about the Biddle brothers and Kate Soffel." She noticed his blank look and continued. "The two brothers were in the Allegheny County Jail to be hanged after killing a shop owner and a police officer during a robbery in the early 1900s. Kate Soffel fell in love with one of the brothers and helped them escape. The problem was that Kate was the warden's wife."

"Could be a big problem, I suppose. Who do I play? What happened to them?"

"You play Ed, the handsome, charismatic brother that Kate fell in love with. The brothers were shot and killed during the escape, and Kate was wounded. Her husband divorced, and disowned her and she served time in prison for helping the brothers escape. Not a happy ending for any of them."

"Hmmmmmmm. This is a true story, then?"

"Uh-huh. It happened in 1902." Maggie tried to hide a yawn. "Well, then, let's try to get a little more sleep. There will be plenty for me to do tomorrow. We can talk more then, too." Maggie crawled back into the comforter and pulled it around her.

"Goodnight, Maggie. Thank you. You took a risk taking a strange man into your home, even if he was injured."

Tyler took her hand and squeezed it gently. Maggie felt warm and tingly all over and squeezed back.

"Goodnight, Tyler. Sleep well."

Neither stirred for the rest of the night.

Maggie woke feeling slightly chilled, and checking the fire, saw that it was almost out. She got out of her warm cocoon and stirred the embers, added kindling to get the flames started again and then began to add logs to the fire. In no time, she had a steady blaze and began to think about coffee. She opened the door to the pot-bellied stove and used a piece of kindling to light it.

"Good morning, Maggie."

The voice was stronger than last night. Maggie saw that his color was back to normal as well. He kept his eyes on her face and Maggie felt somewhat unsettled. He seemed to be trying to ask her something.

"Are you okay?"

"I feel pretty good considering. But, uh, um...do you think you could help me up? I need to use the bathroom." Tyler began to put aside the comforter and sit up. He didn't seem to be dizzy with the movement, but Maggie hurried to his side anyway.

"Take it slowly now, let me help you." She helped him up and walked with him to the bathroom. "If you feel dizzy, don't walk out by yourself, call me. If you fall, I may not be able to pick you up."

He grinned at her as he closed the bathroom door. Maggie left him in the bathroom with a washcloth and towel then went back to put coffee on and make pancakes. The coffee was perking and the griddle was heating when Tyler walked slowly back into the room.

Maggie looked over at him and smiled. "I'll have breakfast ready in a few minutes, have a seat. Do you want coffee?"

"Yeah, black, please. Can I help?" Tyler walked toward her and looked over her shoulder at the pancakes. He looked at the pancake mix and the bag of chocolate chips that were on the counter. "Are you putting *chocolate chips* in the pancakes?" He sounded horrified and Maggie laughed.

"You can't help, just sit down and drink your coffee. Of course those are chocolate chips! Chocolate is the fifth basic food group. It's also a great stress reliever." She poured a cup of coffee and handed it to him. "I can make yours without the chocolate if you prefer."

"I think I can live dangerously. Bring on the chocolate!" Tyler laughed, but grimaced, took his coffee over to the table and sat down gingerly holding his head. "Don't make me laugh, it hurts too much," but he grinned at her as he continued to sip the coffee.

Maggie piled pancakes on a plate and bought them over to the table. Taser danced around her feet as she carried the plate. She forked several of them onto

Tyler's plate and then sat down at her place and took a pancake without chocolate chips for Taser who inhaled it and looked for more.

"Taser, you are such a fraud! No more, go eat your kibble."

Taser skulked off and began to eat as if were starving. For several minutes, neither of them spoke watching his antics.

"Taser, isn't that an unusual name for a German Shepard?"

"Yes, but it suits him, he's my protector."

Silence fell again as they finished the pancakes and coffee. When all of the pancakes had disappeared, Tyler leaned over.

"I'm in your debt, you know. Not everyone would have taken a stranger into their home and cared for them, especially in the middle of nowhere. Not to mention losing sleep to make sure I was all right."

"There is no debt. I'm only glad I was able to help you. Besides, I'm not totally naïve; I have ways of protecting myself." Maggie got up from the table and began clearing the dishes but Tyler stopped her by taking her hand.

"Go do what you planned for the cabin. I'm able to clear the table and wash a few dishes. Headache's better and I *can* wash a few dishes. So, go, do what you need to do."

Maggie's breathing had sped up along with her heartrate when he touched her. She hoped that nothing showed on her face about how she was feeling. This was so much better than the daydreams she had about Tyler Sinclair. She had such a crush on him and he was so much more in real life.

She took a deep breath and looked into Tyler's face, it was smiling up at her so she smiled back and said, "Are you sure you feel all right? Because I should really get up to the loft and check the roof to see if there's any damage from the tree."

Tyler convinced her he was fine to wash the dishes.

"Okay. Don't stay up too long and if you need me for anything give a holler, I'll hear you."

Tyler leaned forward as if to kiss her but continued to bend over the table to pick up the dishes. Maggie strode away getting her toolbox, silently calling herself every kind of fool for thinking he was about to kiss her.

Tyler watched her walk away and finished clearing the table. He kicked himself for not kissing her. Each time she touched him he felt an awareness go through him. He didn't think she would welcome any romantic moves on his part; she'd give him that smile and tell him that he needed to rest and get his strength back. He hated to tell her that he thought he had his strength back, at least in some parts of his anatomy. But more to the point, he needed to remember what happened to him before he started anything with her. Even though Maggie said she knew who he was, he wasn't sure why someone would hurt him. He was an actor, not some gangster, for crying out loud! How did he get here, the middle of nowhere in a blizzard? Until he was sure about everything, he wasn't in any position to get involved with her.

As Tyler washed the dishes, Maggie was in the loft with a flashlight looking for any signs of damage to the roof. Finding none, she gave a brief prayer of thanks that she wasn't going to have to sink more money into the lodge. She should just sell it, but it was part of her family, and it made her feel connected to them somehow, as did the old Victorian she lived in that had also belonged to her great-great-grandparents. Maggie sat on the floor and thought about her life and how screwed up it was. By this time, she thought she would be married with some kids and a dog or two, not an old maid who worked most of the holidays because her coworkers begged her to work them so they could be with their families. Maggie had never been dissatisfied with her life before; she accepted who she was and truly loved her career. She just knew she was missing something in her life, but tried not to dwell on that. Once she thought she had that "something"…but she was mistaken.

She'd been astounded when David Willis asked her out. He was a fellow in neurosurgery, and she had given him directions to the on-call room when he got lost in the maze of the surgical wing. He asked her to join him for coffee the next day after their shifts had ended and they talked for hours. They went out for dinner a few nights later when they found that they both had the night off. She may have been a little disappointed when he hadn't kissed her goodnight, but she soon got over it when he called her forty-five minutes later when he got home. They again talked for hours until two in the morning. She went to sleep thinking that maybe David could be "the one."

The next several months went by in a haze of romantic euphoria. David was attentive and after a few weeks, they made love for the first time. Although it was a rather disappointing first time for Maggie, David seemed satisfied, and Maggie thought that maybe it was her lack of experience that was making this less than perfect; it would get better and more exciting for her when she got used to making love. They still went out regularly, but the sex never seemed to get better for Maggie; David seemed to enjoy it, though. Maggie began to think that there might be something wrong with her; David seemed happy enough and she was looking forward to spending the rest of her life with him. She had never really sought out a doctor to date, although she heard stories of how difficult it was to work with them once the relationship soured, as it usually did. She wasn't sure what she would do if things didn't work out, which they would.

Linda also worked in the operating room and was from the eastern part of the state. When she had been complaining about how hard it was to find a decent roommate or rent that was not an arm and a leg, Maggie offered to have her come and live with her. The old Victorian that Maggie's grandparents had left to her was huge. Her great-great-grandfather had built and then lovingly maintained the house when he married her great-great-grandmother, and Maggie's great-grandparents, grandparents, and parents had followed suit. They got along quite well; both knew when to let the other alone or when to socialize. In good weather, they were able to walk to the hospital, and shopping was not that far away.

They didn't see that much of each other; Linda was a social butterfly and was making her way through the surgical staff like there was no tomorrow. She never brought any of them to the house in the two years she'd lived there, however, and Maggie was grateful for that.

One evening, Maggie was late getting home because she was on call for the transplant team and there was a donor heart coming in for one of their patients. She was supposed to have dinner with David that evening and she had called and told him she would have to pass due to the surgery. The transplant surgery was cancelled when the potential recipient developed a fever. She got home and David's car was in the drive. She let herself in, happily anticipating that David was waiting for her to get home, no matter how late that was. When she came in the door, she heard David and Linda talking.

"When are you going to tell her about us?" asked a strident and demanding voice.

"Linda, it isn't that easy. I do care about Maggie—she's a wonderful person. She wouldn't understand any of this. I didn't plan on falling for you while I was seeing her."

"David, I don't want to hurt her either but the longer you put it off, the more it's going to hurt her. How long do you think we can hide this?"

Maggie never did hear what David had to say to that as she walked into the living room trying to hold on to whatever dignity she could salvage, especially seeing them wrapped around each other on the sofa. She steeled herself to get through the next several minutes without falling apart. As much as she wanted to scream at both of them, she couldn't get her voice above a whisper.

"Hello, David, Linda. I don't think there is anything either of you can say, I heard it all. I guess this is what was meant by eavesdroppers never hear anything good.

I suppose this is where you try to say you never meant to hurt me, right, David? I think it's a little late for that; you should have been up front with me when you discovered your feelings for Linda. It would have been better than to walk into my house to this." She waved her hand at the two of them. She kept her hands clenched on her thighs to maintain some control.

"Linda, I think you'll need to find another place to live considering these events, don't you? I'll give you until the end of the week to pack and find a place. Goodnight." She didn't give either of them a chance to say anything, what could they say that hadn't already been said? Maggie kept her head up until she got into her room and then the tears started flowing and she slid down the closed door to the floor hugging her knees to her chest. She had no idea what was going on in the living room; she heard voices, and then the door closing as David left. She heard Linda coming up the stairs and pausing in front of her door but she kept going. Linda had already left for work when Maggie got up the next morning and when Maggie returned home that evening Linda had moved her belongings out. Maggie heard that she moved in with David that day.

She was more embarrassed facing her coworkers. Did any of them know what had been going on? Of course they did. Nothing was private in a hospital. She tried to keep up a strong front at work but she could see the pitying looks her coworkers and even the doctors tried to hide. She knew she wouldn't be able to stay in the OR and began looking for a transfer.

Okay, quit feeling sorry for yourself. So the hunk in the kitchen didn't kiss you. Why would he? He's famous and you are well, just ordinary. Still, she couldn't help daydreaming about Tyler; she could, even now, see his body as she cleaned him up and dressed him. Maggie heard Tyler call up to her so she got up and climbed down the ladder. It was time to get a grip and check her patient.

CHAPTER 4

Tyler had finished the dishes and was sitting on the sofa thinking about what Maggie had told him. He examined his reflection in the mirror when he was in the bathroom that morning. It did look like he'd been beaten up and he felt as if he'd been thrown from then run over by a bull. He didn't think he was the type of person who liked to start fights, and if he really was an actor then he wouldn't likely do anything that would mess his face up to keep him from working, would he? He needed to ask Maggie if he'd been drinking, but she would have said that when he woke up. He could rule that out, he didn't think he got drunk. What had happened to him? He needed to remember.

His thoughts drifted to the woman in the loft. He liked her face, pretty, he thought. He usually preferred blondes, but the way her red hair shone in the firelight made him forget that fact. Her eyes were the color of the melted milk chocolate she used in the pancakes that morning. Was she married? No, there was no ring on that finger. Was there a man in her life? He didn't think so, when they talked about being stranded here, she said no one would look for her until she didn't go to work next week. He wondered about that, how could she not have someone in her life? She was small but not skinny; her curves were in all the right places and were luscious, in spite of the baggy sweatshirt she wore.

He was stranded here for maybe a week, and nothing could be done about it. The company was good and the surroundings comfortable. He just wished he could remember what had happened that landed him here. Maggie had told him not to push it; the memories would come.

He got up, bored with his ruminating, walked to the ladder, and yelled up to Maggie, "Do you need any help up there? I could do with some activity."

"The last thing I need is for you to climb up here, get dizzy, and fall off the loft and break your neck. I'm almost done up here then we can talk about what our options are for getting out of here or calling for help. Just take it easy and get your strength back, Tyler."

A short while later Tyler heard the old ladder creak, and he got up to hold it steady for Maggie as she came down. He noticed the way the old faded jeans clung to her bottom and almost reached out to touch her but held back.

"Hey there, pretty lady, everything all right up there?"

Maggie felt her heart skip when he said that, he was *flirting* with her! She finished coming down the ladder and looked up at his face. "No leaks, only spider webs and mouse droppings! Ugh." She hated the blush she felt on her cheeks but maybe Tyler wouldn't notice or, if he did, he'd think it was from working in the loft. She went to the door and opened it. "The snow's stopped. I'm going out and check the damage to the truck; it might not be as bad as it looked last night." She got her jacket and gloves, and calling to Taser went out to examine the aftermath of last night's storm.

Tyler, growing restless, went looking for his coat; it was hanging by the fire in the bedroom. He gave it a sniff and didn't smell any alcohol on it, he'd been right, he wasn't drunk yesterday. He looked around the room, the northern wall was all glass, and the heavy drapery opened to let in the dim light; if the double fireplace hadn't been burning, he imagined the room would be cold. A huge sleigh bed, across from the windows with dark green furnishings that matched the drapes filled most of the wall. A chest of drawers and a large wardrobe, both intricately carved and apparently seamless, completed the room. He didn't linger long but hurried to join Maggie by the truck surveying the damage.

The damage was as bad as it had looked in the night. The huge, old pine filled what was left of the truck bed, collapsing it flattening the rear tires; the roof of the cab was squashed past the headrests and the steering wheel had broken in half. She tried to reach in through the broken windows to pry the doors open with a crowbar and retrieve her cell phone, but it was useless. After tying to snag the cell phone with the hook on the crowbar, Maggie finally admitted defeat; there was no way to get the phone out of the truck. Maggie sniffed the air for leaking gasoline and checked the surrounding, but it seemed as if the tank was intact. The damage to the porch wasn't too bad; the roof was hanging off the supports at the far corner, falling onto the pickup's hood, crumpling it to the grill.

While Maggie tried to retrieve the phone, Taser was beside himself, bounding through the snow then back to his mistress to have her follow. He took a running start, then dove into the drifts, leading with his nose and slid through the snow. He lifted his head biting at the snow, and shaking it off his muzzle to lick at it. Maggie watched him, shaking her head at his antics but laughing as well. "Silly dog," she would say affectionately.

Tyler found himself watching her, and was entranced with the expressions flitting across her face when she looked at the German Shepard. Her cheeks, flushed from the cold, were pink and the sound of her laughter coursed through him like a melody. God, she was beautiful, and fun, and intelligent, and he found himself growing hard with wanting her. He shifted uncomfortably, trying to ease his suddenly painful erection, when she pelted him with a snowball.

They spent most of the afternoon outside, Maggie throwing snowballs at him and Taser, and watching Taser make snow dog angels. He ran back and forth, trying to catch the snowballs, and barking when he did catch them and they crumbled in his mouth as he bit into them. Both of them were laughing and carrying on like kids, until Maggie noticed that the light was beginning to fade. She called for Taser, and the three of them went back into the lodge.

"I had fun today. I can't remember when I've laughed so hard." Tyler added logs to the fire as he spoke and Maggie was instantly at his side.

"Oh, no! I forgot about your ribs. Are you in pain?"

Tyler shook his head and added some to the potbelly stove to fix dinner. "I'm fine. It only hurts when I laugh and I've quit for now." He grinned at her. "What's on the menu for dinner tonight?" He hoped to divert her attention and sighed in relief when she answered.

"Okay, here's your choices, chili, soup of several different kinds, canned tuna, ham, or chicken, or mac and cheese. Take your pick."

"Such an extensive menu, how about mac and cheese and tuna sandwiches; you made me hungry woman!" Tyler realized how that sounded and seeing Maggie blush again added, "All that running around you did with Taser, I mean. What I mean—"

"I know what you mean." Maggie laughed at his discomfort. "I worked up an appetite as well. Let me wash up and I'll start getting dinner."

Maggie went into the bath, still laughing, but also wishing he meant it the other way then cursing herself for being an idiot. When she returned to the kitchen, Tyler had already drained the tuna and had the water on the stove to boil for the macaroni.

"You're pretty handy to have around sir. You seem to know your way around a kitchen."

"My mom made sure we all knew how to cook and do laundry. She said she wouldn't be around forever and especially not when we went off to school. I remember that anyway. Where's the bread, and what do you want me to mix with the tuna?" Maggie pointed out the cupboard where the bread and packets of mayonnaise and pickle relish were stored. "It's easier to buy packets of mayo than the jars for up here, they don't need refrigerated."

Tyler and Maggie worked together fixing dinner, Tyler poured kibble into Taser's bowl, and watched as he attacked it as if he hadn't eaten in a month. When he finished, he circled the rug by the fireplace several times, then plopped down with a bang and curled up to go to sleep.

"What was that? He seemed to just pick up all four paws and fall to the floor."

Maggie laughed. "He does that all the time, you get used to the noise. The first time he did it as a puppy, I thought he hurt himself."

Tyler thought he might like getting used to Taser's way of going to sleep if it meant being around Maggie and her musical laughter. He shook himself wondering where that thought had come from.

They ate dinner talking about nothing and everything. They talked about music, and found that they liked many of the same kinds but, where Maggie liked country, Tyler liked Irish punk rock, they both agreed on classic rock and opera. Tyler's taste in books seemed to be similar to Maggie's, they both liked suspense and mysteries. They talked while they cleared away dinner, and continued until the fire light began to dim and Maggie couldn't hide her yawns any longer.

"I think I'll turn in. It was a long night; I didn't sleep much after the tree crashed. Look, why don't you take the bed, I fit on the sofa better, and we both need a goodnight's sleep."

"You're right, we both need a goodnight's sleep, but that bed looks more than big enough for both of us. I've been sitting on the sofa; it isn't that comfortable, so I can imagine the kind of sleep you'll get on it. Besides, I have the feeling your chaperone will be joining us, he seems the type to be spoiled enough to sleep in a bed and not the hearth rug." Tyler tried to make his voice sound as if this was not big deal, but he wanted to be close to this woman.

Maggie laughed, and agreed that before too long Taser would be crawling up into the bed. She was tired, and the sofa really was not a great place to sleep; she'd fallen asleep on it and awakened stiff and sore.

As soon as she and Tyler got into the bed, Taser came bounding in and jumped up onto the bed. He did his turning around and then dropped onto the mattress at their feet. He no sooner hit the bed than the soft sounds of doggy snoring were heard.

"Welcome to the wonderful world of Maggie," she said to Tyler. "I hope you have enough room and blankets, Taser can get kinda greedy at night. He thinks everything I own really belongs to him."

"I think I like being part of your world. I'm quite comfortable. Goodnight, Maggie, sleep tight." Tyler rolled over, hoping he would get some sleep with Maggie so close.

Having Tyler so near was disturbing for her as well. She'd had a crush on this man for years without ever meeting him, and now here he was in her bed, albeit innocently. She wished she were one of those gorgeous Hollywood types, who could sweep him off his feet and make him want her as much as she wanted him. She tried not to toss and turn for fear of waking him, but couldn't get her thoughts to be still. She tried to convince herself it was just her crush on him but after getting to know him today, she was afraid it was becoming more than that. She really liked him. Maybe once he was back in his real world, and remembered what happened, he would be a different person and she wouldn't like him; maybe he was a real jerk in reality. Yeah, and maybe, Taser could speak English! After a long while, Maggie fell asleep.

Tyler knew she wasn't sleeping, he could hear her brain working. What was she thinking? He figured it was something about him. Was she afraid he'd become some sort of sex maniac and attack her? Well, he *was* thinking of sex, but the long sweet kind where she wanted him as much as he wanted her. What was it about her that attracted him so much? God knew he'd been with prettier and more glittering women. There was something about her, he couldn't quite put his finger on it, he'd think about it tomorrow, he was too tired now. Shortly after hearing Maggie's breathing even out, that told him she was at last sleeping, he let himself sleep as well.

CHAPTER 5

Tyler had been sitting on the sofa, opposite the fire and petting Taser. He'd been drifting, watching the flames, and feeling pretty good in spite of his injuries. The headache was down to an intermittent throb and he no longer felt nauseated, something he had never told Maggie. He thought he'd surprise Maggie with fixing lunch for the both of them. She was outside getting wood. As he stood up, he had a flash of memory.

He was free for the day, and driving around Pittsburgh just looking around. He had stopped at a traffic light when the car behind hit his. Ty looked in the rear mirror, and saw that the driver was getting out, so he got out as well. "It doesn't look like there's any damage. I don't think we need to worry about it." The other driver was built like a gorilla. He had a scarf wrapped around his lower face and a knit cap pulled over his forehead, he came toward Tyler as he started to get back into the car. He moved his arm so that Tyler could see the barrel of a gun. "What the hell...," Tyler started to say.

"You're going to come with us. I don't want to use this, but I have no problem with it. Don't push me."

Tyler continued to edge toward his car slowly, and started to reach behind him for the door, when the goon hit him with the butt of the gun. As Tyler slumped forward, the massive oaf grabbed him and dragged him to the other car. He was pushed unceremoniously into the back seat, and once the gorilla got in they took off.

Who were they? What did they want with him? Ty had no idea. He got up slowly and walked to the bathroom. As he looked at his reflection in the mirror, he noted that his face was flushed and wet with perspiration. He turned on the tap, and rinsed his face with the icy water to clear his head. When he lifted his head and looked in the mirror again, he realized that he did know this face and he was who Maggie said he was. That brief flash was a start, should he tell Maggie about it? Would the idea of a gunman forcing him into a car frighten her? He decided he would take his chance, and tell her that he was beginning to remember. He went back to the living room, gazed at the fire, and put another log on. He sat down and thought about Maggie.

She wasn't leading lady beautiful, but there was something about her, as if she was lit up from inside. She was resourceful, he was proof of that, for such a little thing she managed to get him into her truck and then into the lodge. She was caring; didn't she help him when she knew nothing about him and how he got there? He loved the way her hair changed colors in the firelight, all red and brown and flecked with gold. And her eyes, a man could get lost in those soft chocolatey-brown depths. He liked the way they crinkled when she smiled up at him. She didn't do that often enough he thought, he'd like to change that, she should smile often and laugh more.

Maggie came in with an armful of wood, and immediately knew something wasn't right. She dumped the wood on the floor and rushed over to him. "What's wrong, are you okay?" Maggie saw that he was flushed and reached up to touch his forehead, "No fever, what happened? Are you in pain, can't breathe, what?" Her words ran together as she looked for a physical reason for his obvious disquiet.

Ty took hold of her hands. "Hey, I'm fine; I just had a memory, that's all. It was…unsettling." Tyler drew Maggie down to the sofa. He told her what he had just remembered, and that he knew for certain who he was. "I wonder how I managed to get away, or did they just leave me in the woods?"

Maggie sat listening to him, certain that he was lucky to have survived. She kept her hands in his larger ones, and felt that his pulse was much steadier than hers was right now. "What do you think they wanted? Do you think they knew who you were or was it just a random act?"

"I'm not sure; they didn't say my name, or anyone's in the car. I don't know what it was. I'd only got in late the night before, so not too many people knew I was here yet. I arrived early so I could look around before I started shooting."

"Anyone involved with the movie that could want you out of the way? WAIT! What about ransom or insurance or something like that?" Maggie was practically jumping on the sofa in excitement with her idea. "I've seen movies where the producer or director or someone needed money, so he sabotaged the movie by taking out the star to collect the insurance."

"Maggie, Maggie, slow down, honey. You've been seeing way too many mystery movies. That doesn't happen in real life. Besides, we don't know if it *is* related to the movie or just a random carjacking."

"But YOU got the part, so you're the one at risk right now. Can you remember anything else?"

Tyler shook his head, and said he hadn't even been trying to remember, the images just came to him. Maggie let the matter drop, she said she was hungry, and was going to fix lunch. Tyler stopped her and said that he had it under control.

"Canned ham and hotcakes. I even put chocolate chips in the hotcakes because I know chocolate is a necessity you can't live without."

Ty reached down and taking Maggie's hand, led her over to the kitchen area. Maggie was confused and overwhelmed at the way Tyler was behaving, not like a famous person who appeared in the tabloids with a different woman on his arm, but like real person. One who didn't expect to be waited on, and pitched in to help out. As they ate lunch, Ty noticed her brow all scrunched together and asked her what she was thinking.

Maggie told him what she had been puzzling over as they fixed lunch and Tyler just shook his head at her. "I didn't expect you to help around her, cooking I mean. After all, this isn't the kind of place you're used to. Don't you have maids and cooks and such, to do all this for you?"

"Honey, my parents raised us to do chores around the house, I didn't start out being an actor or famous." He laughed openly at her. "Only difference is that my job puts me up as a bigger-than-life persona. People respond to the persona, not the *person*. Don't believe everything that's in the tabloids. You expected me to have you cater to me and not pitch in, right? I let you do that yesterday, when I couldn't get my bearings, but I'm feeling much now, and I need to do something. It's not my nature to have people wait on me, my mother didn't raise any of us to be like that. Now, finish your lunch. The sun's out, and I thought that maybe we could take Taser out for a bit. What do you think?"

Maggie could feel herself blush as he said all this to her and felt like an idiot. "I'm such an ass. That is pretty much what I thought. You must think I'm an idiot."

Tyler only took her hand in his and held it to his lips and kissed it. "No, I think you're pretty terrific."

They finished lunch, and cleaned up; all the while Tyler kept talking trying to get Maggie to loosen up some.

They took Taser out, but stayed on the porch watching as he repeated his dive-bomber antics of yesterday. Maggie again brought up her theory of a kidnapping plot.

"Tyler, just because I read mysteries doesn't mean that this couldn't be real. Who knew you were coming in a day or two early, just to look around? You said only a few people knew that, who were they?"

Tyler realized that it would be much easier to go along with Maggie's conspiracy theory so he told her the three people who knew he would be in Pittsburgh before he was scheduled to begin shooting. "Mike Andrews, my agent, for one. I don't think he would arrange to have me kidnapped; he only gets paid if I'm working. Then there was Sal Neville, the director, we've worked together before, I trust him, he's an actor's director. And then, Sal's assistant, Terri Morgan; I don't know her, she's only been with Sal about two months. Of course the hotel staff knew I'd arrived when I checked in."

"Mmmmmmmmmmm. Terri may be the one; she started working for Sal about the time he announced he was signed on to do this project. Could she have some reason for getting you out of the way?"

"How do you know all that?"

"Since the movie's being made here, there was a big press conference announcing it. Sal was here, along with the head of the Film Office in Pittsburgh, plus, I'm on the medical team for the Film Office. So who is she, and how would she benefit if you weren't here?"

"I don't know; I've never met her. We're not sure she or anyone else is behind this, Maggie. It could have just been a random act. And Maggie, only my mother calls me Tyler and that's just when she's upset or angry at me. Everyone calls me Ty." He grinned at her, hoping to distract her from her theory of him being personally in danger.

"Humph, and pigs fly!" However, she let the matter drop, and called Taser to go back into the cabin; where Ty added a log or two to the fire. While the canned milk was heating, she rummaged through one of the cupboards, built into the mantle, and dragged out and old chess set. "I read somewhere that you play. How about a game?"

"Sure. I'll even let you take white, since I'm such a nice guy." He grinned at her, and she rolled her eyes at him.

Maggie made the cocoa while Ty set up the board, they spent the next several hours playing a very evenly matched game.

"Usually I don't meet many people outside my family that can keep me on my toes," Ty told her.

"My grandfather taught me to play, she didn't believe in letting kids win to make them feel good. When I was finally able to beat him, I knew I had done it all on my own. He was puffed up with pride at my accomplishment." Maggie smiled wistfully at the memory.

While they played, Ty asked her to tell him the story of Mrs. Soffel and the Biddle Brothers, as he couldn't remember anything about the movie he was here to film.

"It started in April of 1901. Ed and Jack Biddle, along with two women and another man, planned to rob a grocer who, it was rumored, kept a great deal of money in his house. There are a couple of versions to how it went down but either way, the grocer was killed, and the gang left empty handed. During their getaway, they shot and killed a police officer. They were captured a few days later and went to trial; both were found guilty of murder, and sentenced to be hanged.

"Kate Soffel was the warden's wife; by all accounts she was not a pretty woman, being described as being bucktoothed and hunchbacked. But, her family had political connections, and Peter Soffel was ambitious; he didn't plan on remaining warden forever. She was often seen at the jail, reading the Bible to the inmates, or bringing them fresh baked goods from her kitchen. Ed was supposedly extremely handsome, some stories said he had to have some power over people, and certainly, Kate fell under his spell. She made several visits to the jail, bringing books and special treats she baked especially for him and Jack. Eventually, he convinced her that the brothers were innocent, and she agreed to help them escape. On the pretext of visiting her sister, who lived in nearby McKeesport, she purchased saw blades and revolvers, and smuggled them into their cells. They managed to cut through the bars, and on the night of January 30, Kate either told her husband she was going to visit her sister in McKeesport, or she used chloroform to knock him out, the story's hazy on this part. In reality, she was planning to run away with Ed.

"They made their escape, and traveled north to Perrysville, where they hid in an old schoolhouse; they stole a sled, and began going north toward Butler heading for the Canadian border. The police caught up with them the next afternoon, and during the shootout both brothers were fatally wounded; they died the following day. Kate was also shot, but recovered and served time in prison. Her husband divorced and disowned her, and resigned as warden of the jail. That put a crimp in his political ambitions. He took the children and moved to Ohio where he remarried."

Ty listened to the story, when Maggie finished said, "It makes a good story. Lots of action and romance. Where are we filming this?"

"Mostly in the downtown area; at the old county jail and courthouse. It's a historical landmark now. It closed to prisoners in 1990. It's such an imposing structure that some of the filming will be done around it." The light was beginning to fade and Maggie turned on the lamps. Taser came trotting over to his dish looking for food. "I guess it is time for dinner, you hungry, Ty?"

"Yeah, let me help."

Ty opened a can of chili to heat, as Maggie mixed the biscuits dough to go with it. Maggie added wood to the stove, and put the biscuits in to bake. Ty set the table and put kibble in Taser's bowl. It all seemed so normal and domestic; Maggie felt a shiver up her spine as she watched Ty talk to Taser. He sat at the kitchen table as if he had always been there and felt completely at home there. Desire and longing swept through her as she watched him. Tears burned behind Maggie's eyes, and she hurriedly wiped them away as she bent to open the stove and remove the biscuits.

"Dinner's ready." She brought the basket of biscuits to the table, and then the bowls of chili.

They ate in silence, watching Taser as he wolfed down his food, and came to the table looking for handouts, which Ty surreptitiously gave him under the table. Maggie pretended not to notice.

They both cleared the table, Maggie washed while Ty dried the dishes. Maggie felt herself drawn even more to Ty the longer she spent with him. She was afraid she was falling in love with him and decided to put some distance between them. She told Ty she had a headache, and didn't feel like playing chess tonight.

Maggie sat in the big armchair, her legs hanging over one arm and her head cradled on the other by the hearth, alternately staring into space then into the flames. It was no good; she had fallen for the handsome actor. In order to save her pride, she could never let him know how he affected her. She daydreamed about what it would be like if Ty loved her as well. "Stop it! There's no use wishing or daydreaming." Taser seemed to sense her mood, because he came over put his head on her lap and licked her hand. She petted him and kissed his nose. Satisfied that all was well with his world, he lay down in front of the chair after doing his usual three turns and lifting all four paws to plop down. "Silly dog," Maggie said to him, absently, and continued to stare at the fire.

She must've dozed because she came awake with a start.

"Shhh, it's only me. I was going to the bathroom, and saw that you were asleep. I didn't want to disturb you," Tyler said as he draped the afghan over her.

"I guess I fell asleep sitting here. Happens to me a lot. You okay?" Maggie pulled the afghan tightly around her, more for protection than warmth.

"I was going to ask you the same thing. What's wrong, Maggie? You seemed different after dinner. Is it something I've done?"

Maggie looked at his face, examined his eyes, and knew she wasn't going to tell him she wanted him. What was she to do; he sensed something was wrong she had to say something. Thinking quickly she said, "I've been remembering something from the night of the storm. With everything that happened after I brought you here, I forgot about it until just a little while ago. You remember when you told me about what happened to you? When I was driving up here, I saw tire tracks. They must've been in front of me all along, but the only reason I noticed them was that the snow was churned up, as if the car had been stuck and spun its wheels to get traction. There were footprints there, too. It looked like two people were pushing the car. There was another set too, moving toward the woods; I think they were yours. What if whoever kidnapped you comes back to look in the woods, looking for you, they'll come here eventually, it's the only shelter in several miles. Taser will give us some warning that strangers are nearby, but we need to think of a plan." Maggie was impressed with herself for thinking of this, maybe she had been thinking of this in the back of her mind all along after Ty told her what had happened.

"I hadn't thought about that or of putting you in any danger. How far is it to the village? I'll walk out of here in the morning." The thought of something happening to Maggie was an anathema to him, but he didn't want to leave her, either. He felt something for her, he wanted a chance to explore that.

"You'll do no such thing. Like I said, we're pretty isolated back here. I was just thinking out loud. There's been so much fresh snow since then, my tire tracks are probably not visible anymore, and the turnoff to the drive is difficult to find, even in good weather. Your tracks are surely gone by now even if the tire marks aren't. You're safe with me. Besides, I know how to use that rifle over the mantle."

Ty nodded. "Okay, that's good to know. We are pretty isolated with the blizzard, and not able to get your phone. If someone is searching, won't they see the smoke from the fireplace?"

Maggie thought about that. "No, we're pretty far back from the road. The ceiling is so low with those dark clouds that the smoke will probably be missed."

Tyler reached out to her. "Since you're awake, come to bed. I added logs to the fire already." He reached out to her, she reluctantly put her hand in his, and together they went to bed.

Maggie had no trouble going back to sleep. When she woke again, the sun was just starting to become visible through the window.

"It's just after seven, why not sleep a little longer?" Ty asked as he rolled over to face her. He put his arm around her, and pulled her toward him, so her head was on his uninjured side.

It felt so good she could lie here forever with him. She closed her eyes, drank in the scent of him, and sighed. It was no use, she had fallen for Ty; she was only going to be devastated when he went back to his life, and she went back to hers. She was smart enough to realize that this was a period out of time, he wouldn't know she was alive when they got back to Pittsburgh, and his life as a famous actor. She was going to have to put some distance between them, that was the only way to protect herself, she realized.

"Do I really want to protect myself? Ty seems to want me as much as I want him. Why not go for it? Let me be loved by someone like Ty, if only for this short time. I'll be able to remember him for the rest of my life." Concluding her inner dialogue, she resolved to accept whatever happened. If he made any move toward her, she would accept willingly. She got up, and after brushing her teeth and washing her face, prepared to make coffee. And she waited for Ty to make a move.

CHAPTER 6

The next few days passed in much the same way. Maggie spent the mornings making minor repairs, securing the shutters and caulking around the windows and doors, to keep out the wintery air. She cut firewood, and tried to brace the porch roof up with some of the longer logs in an attempt to keep it from falling down completely. In the afternoons, she and Ty played outside with Taser. They played chess in the evenings, after dinner by the fire, or read the books that were on the shelves. Maggie was falling more in love with him with each passing day. Still, Ty hadn't made a move. Maybe she was mistaken; he only saw her as his rescuer and perhaps a friend. Or, maybe he wanted her to make the first move.

On Friday, while they played chess, Ty asked her, "Why aren't you married or at least seriously involved with someone?"

Maggie's expression became tight, as she returned, "What makes you think I'm not?"

"You've never mentioned anyone being anxious about you, or looking for you, other than the people you work with when you don't show up for work on Sunday. Who was he?"

"Who was who?"

"The man who made you avoid any romantic relationships. Don't tell me there wasn't someone. I've seen you, when you let your guard down with me, you laugh and tease me, then you close up when I get too close. I'm attracted to you, and I think you are attracted to me, even if you won't admit it."

"Of all the conceited actorish behaviors!" Maggie sputtered and tried again. "I'm attracted to you? You really are delusional, that bump on your head was worse than I thought."

"Maggie, honey, c'mon. Be honest to yourself at least. I'm going to be honest with you. I am attracted to you. I have been since I woke up and saw those amazing chocolatey-brown eyes. The more I try to get close to you, the more walls you put up when you remember to be on guard. It can't be because you don't feel anything for me, so it has to be from someone in your past. Or — is it me? You said that you were surprised that I helped, so is it because of who I am? You believe the tabloids about how many women I'm seen with, how I sleep with all of them? I'm not a womanizer, Maggie. Tell me you want me too; let me show you I'm not like that." Ty came over to her chair, pulled her up, and led her to the sofa. He pulled her close to him, and enveloped her in his arms. "I've wanted to do this since Monday," he murmured. His lips touched hers as he kissed her and held her close. His lips felt like heaven to her. His kiss became more as she relaxed against him, he licked the seam of her mouth with his tongue. He took her bottom lip between his teeth and nibbled. She moaned against him, and kissed him back, opening her mouth to him welcoming his exploration and deepening the kiss. Finally, the kiss ended, and Tyler pulled a breathless Maggie down to the sofa, where he just held her close to his side.

They sat like that for a long while until Maggie said, "His name's David." She told him all about him. How he and Linda made her feel like a joke for believing him, and his declarations of love. How she felt as if the whole operating room staff knew what had happened, laughing at her behind her back; or worse, pitying her. "I transferred to the emergency department a month later. I couldn't take it any longer, the laughing or the pity."

"So you hid yourself away all this time, waiting for me to come along." He laughed against her hair. "You are a beautiful, amazing woman. You light up a room. I like that you're smart, witty, funny, and extremely independent. You know your own mind, and you stand up for yourself. This isn't the best time…hell, there may never be a best time for this, but I am falling in love with you. When this is all over, getting out of here, the movie, finding out what happened to me, we'll need to make plans; we can't lose each other." Ty nudged her until she was sitting on his lap. He held her face in his hand and kissed her nose, her eyes, and finally, her mouth.

The minute Ty's lips found hers, she could think of nothing else but the heat that blazed within her. She refused to think that his declaration was in reaction to the situation they found themselves in; she had heard that feelings developed in the midst of a misadventure never lasted; this could certainly be classified as a misadventure. Maggie trembled at his touch, and felt the unshed tears burning her eyes and throat. Ty's tongue gently probed the seam of her lips, her mouth opened to his as the kiss deepened. She found herself opening to him with a breathy gasp when their tongues touched, first hesitantly, then with growing need and heat.

Then Maggie's hands wrapped around his neck as she kissed him, meeting each thrust of his tongue with her own, becoming a little more sure of herself, because of how he was reacting to her response. Her fingers threaded through his hair as she held his head closer to her to deepen the kiss. She felt the heat of desire course through her. David's kisses had never made her feel this way. She wanted time to stop so she could kiss Ty forever. His arm tightened around her as he deepened the kiss, his tongue invading her mouth and dueling with her tongue. He tasted wonderful, and she threw herself into the kiss. If only kissing him made her feel like this, what would full-blown sex do to her? She'd explode she decided, into tiny little pieces.

Ty's mouth lifted for a second, moved to kiss her neck, and Maggie's head fell back to give him more access, as he heard a soft moan escape her. She could feel her nipples tighten in reaction to his kisses, she could feel her insides clutch with a sharp, fierce need that was unfamiliar to her. She took his face in her hands and brought his mouth back to hers. As she strained to get closer to Ty her brain, which had stopped working at the first touch of his lips, suddenly reengaged itself and she now pulled away.

Ty leaned back to look into her eyes. He saw the unshed tears there as well as apprehension; but he also saw passion there. He was encouraged by the passion, but needed to address the tears and fear he felt in her. Ty wiped her eyelids with his thumbs, where tears were threatening to spill over. "What's wrong? You don't like the way I kissed you? You're not attracted to me? We don't have to do this I'm not pushing you into anything." Ty tried to keep his voice soft, but the burning need he felt made sound husky and harsh. He cursed himself for that, hoping Maggie wouldn't be disgusted with the timbre of his words.

"No, oh, God, no! I'm just not very good at this, and it was so, so terrific. No, that's not the word I want to use either. Magical, breathtaking, mind-blowing might come close. You just made me feel, I don't know, wonderful, and beautiful, and very desirable. I can't begin to tell you how often I've daydreamed about you, and here you are kissing me." By now, tears were streaming down Maggie's cheeks. "Don't pay any attention to me; I don't know what I mean. I'm just overwhelmed by you," she hesitated, "by this." She waved her hand between them to indicate her meaning.

Ty pulled her back to his lap, nibbled on her bottom lip and waited for her to kiss him. As much as he wanted her, he thought it best to let her set the pace. Hesitating, Maggie took his face in her hands and looked into his eyes; she seemed to find what she had been looking for, because she lowered her mouth to his and kissed him, running her tongue along his lips and softly biting his lower lip. The kiss deepened and Ty, not able to hold back any longer took control. He shifted so that they were both sitting on the sofa then he gently pushed Maggie down until she was lying on the cushions. Her hands were around his neck, her fingers tangling in his hair. Ty slid beside her so his weight was mostly on the sofa, his hand lifting Maggie's T-shirt up and caressed the skin on her belly followed by his mouth and tongue. He felt Maggie tremble beneath him as his hand moved over her.

Maggie's hands moved down to the hem of his shirt and pushed it up, to feel the muscles of his back ripple beneath her fingers. She arched her hips toward him in a silent plea. Ty unzipped her jeans and slid his hand down to touch the moist heat of her core. Maggie gasped as her hips bucked to meet his hand, and pulled his head up to reach his mouth with hers.

As their lips touched, Ty gasped as well but not from Maggie's reaction, there was a cold, wet nose burrowing under his arm toward Maggie's midriff. Maggie bucked harder at the contact and Ty fell off the sofa, both of them laughing.

"I guess Taser wanted some loving as well, he seemed to feel left out," Ty choked out.

"Well, he does seem to have rather good timing. I don't think either one of us is ready for this yet." Maggie rolled off the sofa and helped Ty to his feet. When he tried to talk about what had just happened, Maggie cut him off. "Ty, it's fine. This isn't something I want to rush into. Am I sorry it started? No, but let's wait until we're back in the real world, okay? This might just be a reaction to what's happened and being stuck here together." She didn't look upset, just resolved.

He took her slim body close to him and kissed her hair. "This isn't over, not by a longshot. I'm not giving up on us."

Maggie smiled up at him coquettishly and replied, "Good, I don't want you to."

The rest of the day was spent much like the others, eating, talking, watching Taser play in the snow, then curling up together in front of the fire. As the daylight faded, Maggie began to pack stuff. Tomorrow was Saturday and the possibility of rescue the next day. She wanted to be ready to leave as soon as someone came to get them.

Maggie fell asleep in Ty's arms. Sometime during the night, they both woke up, reaching for each other, touching and kissing. As Ty's hand roamed over Maggie's body, touching her bare skin, he felt her tense then relax into him. He pulled her closer, allowing his leg move up toward the heat of Maggie's core. She began to move against his leg, rubbing harder as she tried to get closer to him. He felt her moist heat along his leg and pressed closer against her.

Tyler's lips found hers, and his tongue explored her hot mouth, dueling with hers. He nipped her bottom lip and moved to her neck, kissing his way down her body as his hands moved her shirt up to expose her breasts. His fingers caressing her nipples caused her to moan beneath him. His mouth closed over a nipple, sucking and teasing it with his teeth, until she writhed and bucked against him. Her hands moved down his back to explore under his shirt, she felt the muscles of his back bunch, as he moved against her.

Tyler continued to move down her body until his mouth found her core. She pushed against his head trying to stop him. "Shhhh, don't, let me love you. You are so beautiful here. Let me love you." His voice vibrated against her sensitive flesh, making her shiver. He kissed his way down her slit and let his tongue swirl around her clitoris.

She squirmed and moaned, there was nothing she could compare it to. Her fingers gripped his hair and held him close as his tongue drove inside her. She felt the coiling get tighter, the heat and moisture oozed seductively from her as Ty continued to move his tongue in and out of her. She knew she was pulling on his hair, but couldn't stop as she continued to pull him closer to her as her hips rubbed herself over his face. Finally, the ratcheting sensation was so intense she cried out as the coiled spring released, flinging her into a maelstrom of feeling that screamed out of her, leaving her breathless. She lay there limply, breathing harshly, as Ty shifted to lie beside her.

He gathered her to him and smoothed her hair as she put her head on his chest. Her unsteady breath was slowly coming back to normal. She looked up at him and smiled softly. "Wow, that was…wow." She reached up and kissed him, tasting herself on his lips and brushing his erection with her thigh. She moved her hand to circle his length, as her lips met his, squeezing slightly. She moved her hand up to the tip and smoothed the drop of moisture around the mushroomed head of his penis.

He moved her hand. "If you keep this up, I won't last," he said, smiling at her. "I really want to make love to you."

She shifted so that he moved over her, and she moved languidly to allow him access. He positioned himself over her and slowly entered her heated core, groaning as he pushed in slowly.

"You feel so good, so hot and tight; your hot little opening milking me." He pushed in, then pulled almost out and pushed in again.

"Oh, God, I can feel your pulse inside me, I've never felt anything like that. It's so *intimate*." Maggie wrapped her arms around him, moving to meet his every thrust.

Faster and deeper, Ty thrust into her, his breathing ragged. He shifted, pulled her upright so that they were chest to chest, and she was straddling his hips. They moved together, and the tight coiling that Maggie felt before was starting again. She felt Ty grow larger inside her and heard his words of encouragement in her ear.

"That's it, baby. Let yourself go. Come for me." His voice was harsh and tight, as he held onto the last vestiges of control, wanting to feel her release before allowing his own.

She let go and felt herself burst into a million pieces. Ty felt her muscles tighten against him as his testicles drew up and constricted. He felt his release engulf him and his seamen spurt out in streams into her as he cried out his orgasm. He felt as if he would never stop coming, Maggie's muscles continued to ripple against him, continuing to milk him. He held her tight until they both were spent. As they came back to earth, they fell to their sides still wrapped in each other gasping for breath. Neither moved, and they drifted off to sleep still curled in each other's arms.

The weak light from the rising sun threw haloes over the entwined couple on the huge sleigh bed. Maggie stretched, bumping into the hard muscles of the man still sleeping beside her. She felt the ache of unused muscles protesting the activity of last night and early this morning. She blushed at the memory of what they had done with each other, feeling her core tightening in response. The man next to her stirred, reaching out to pull her closer to him. She rolled to take his mouth when her stomach growled. Ty's eyes flew open, a smile crinkled his lips.

He nuzzled her neck. "I was going to go for an encore performance, but I think we need some nourishment instead." He swung his legs over the edge of the bed and bent to pull on his pants. Turning to her, he reached out and tugged on her arm. "The sooner we get our strength back, the sooner we can continue what we started last night." He pulled Maggie from the bed and handed her the shirt and pants that were strewn on the floor.

Maggie blushed as she pulled on her clothes, heading toward the bath, needing a moment alone before she faced him again.

After taking care of morning needs, Maggie headed into the kitchen and found Ty busy with oatmeal and coffee. She grabbed bowls and mugs and moved to the table. Tyler filled the bowls with the hot cereal, then they both sat down to eat. Maggie felt shy, keeping head down over the oatmeal, as she ate. She barely tasted the cereal, eating by rote, until Ty's voice broke into her reverie.

"Maggie, talk to me." She looked up and saw the concern in his eyes. She smiled at him, shaking her head.

"I just feel overwhelmed. I'm not used to waking up with anyone, and I've certainly never had marathon sex before, either." The words tumbled out of her as the color in her face deepened and spread down her neck.

"Maggie, I don't know what to say. Whatever it is, it won't be what I want to say to you. Last night was wonderful; you are so responsive, so passionate. I want to do it again. I want to lose myself in you." His gaze never leaving her face as he spoke, willing he to believe him.

Maggie searched his face, seeing no evidence of deceit, only desire. The sight made her feel tingly, causing her nipples to harden into tight peaks. Ty's eyes moved down to her chest, and inhaled deeply. He took his bowl to the sink, rinsed it, and repeating the action for Maggie's bowl, before taking her hand and leading her back to the bedroom. Tyler tenderly undressed Maggie, kissing each section of exposed skin as he moved down her body. Maggie trembled with the sensation, and caught her breath when Ty reached her core. He pulled Maggie onto the bed and kissed down her taut stomach toward the apex of her thighs. His mouth moved over the swollen clit as his hands spread her allowing a finger to penetrate her hot, moist center. He sucked and stroked until he felt the muscles of her vagina clench, then he moved up her body until he penetrated her with his hard length. Maggie wound her legs around him, pulling him closer to her. She met each of his thrusts, arching up to him and squeezing him, her hands on his buttocks, binding him to her.

His breath hissed out in harsh gasps as he plunged deeper and harder into her. The tightening she felt inside her made her crazed with wanting more, she begged for it breathlessly, calling his name as she met him thrust for thrust. She felt his hand reach between them to rub the hard little nub at her center. The moment his fingers touched her she climaxed with a ferocity she had never experienced before. She exploded into a billion shimmering lights and became weightless in Ty's arms. The spasms went on and on until she finally fell, spent, and breathless under his length. Ty pushed into her again, and with a primal growl emptied himself into her. She felt him pulsate deep inside her as his climax washed over him and was awed by the experience. She had never felt this with David, and she had certainly never witnessed him lose himself like Ty had with her. She marveled at the revelation, caressing Ty's back as his breathing slowed, and he moved to her side drawing her close to him. He caressed her in turn, gently kissed her hair, her temple, her nose, and finally her mouth. Maggie kissed him back and nuzzled into his chest.

They lay like that until the light began to fade and Taser nosed them to remind Maggie that he needed fed. The spell was broken, but Maggie didn't mind, as Ty took her hand and together they headed into the kitchen to feed Taser and themselves.

CHAPTER 7

The storm that had swirled both outside, and in the bedroom finally abated; Sunday morning brought sunny, clear-blue skies. Maggie stretched, and woke slowly, squinting against the bright sunlight streaming through the window. She started to get up, but was held in place by an arm draped around her waist. Maggie turned over to see Ty smiling.

"Good morning." He leaned down and took her mouth in a hungry kiss.

"You *are* here. I thought I dreamt it, yesterday, last night, all of it." She was somewhat disconcerted. "I'm not used to waking up with anyone...except Taser."

"Is it so bad? Waking up with me, I mean?" Ty found that he was pleased that she wasn't used to waking up with a man. He put the thought aside, not wanting to examine that feeling just yet.

"No, it's quite nice, actually, and feels pretty good. Last night was wonderful."

"Well, come here then and let's see if we can repeat it."

"I don't think it's a good idea right now."

Ty moved his hand down her body, and caressed her mound, seeing her wince at the pressure. He thought about the past twenty-four hours, and how many times he took her. "I guess we overdid it a little, huh?"

Maggie nodded, and Ty took her hand and kissed her. "We'll have plenty of time when we get home for encore performances." He kissed her again, and got up walking to the bathroom.

She watched the way his nude body moved as he strode away from her she pinched herself to make sure this was real.

After dressing and eating breakfast, they finished getting the lodge winterized, draining the pipes, and packing Maggie's clothes. They went outside with Taser, holding hands and talking. The day was perfect: cold and crisp. Every few steps they stopped and kissed.

They walked through the woods following tracks made by deer and rabbit. Taser chased a few rabbits, but they managed to find their warren and get away. Maggie was dreading going back to the real world. She was afraid Ty would forget about her once they were rescued. Well, not forget her exactly, but distance himself from her and regret what they shared. Ty was looking forward to getting back. He needed to find out what happened to him, and he wanted to continue what he started with Maggie.

"Someone will be coming soon to get us. I was supposed to be at work at seven. When no one is able to get in touch with me, they'll send the state police up here, figuring I got snowed in. Things are going to be different when we get back. It's been sort of dreamlike this week with you, and last night was perfect." She looked at him as if she were trying to sear him into her memory. "I'm not good at saying goodbye, so can we do it now and get it over with?" Maggie refused to look at him now, keeping her eyes on Taser as he raced through the snow. She wrapped her arms around herself as if trying to hold herself together.

"What in heaven's name are you talking about goodbye? I have no intention of saying goodbye to you now that I've found you. If you want to get rid of me you're the one who will have to do it." Ty grabbed her and pulled her close. "I told you that I love you, I don't say that lightly. In fact, other than my family I've never said it before." Ty let her go, and angrily strode away, leaving Maggie feeling no more of a fool than she deserved.

"Ty wait! I'm sorry. This is just so unreal. I mean, what can you possibly see in me? When you get back to your life and the movie, you'll realize that we are too different. Please, don't drag it out, please."

"Things *are* going to get crazy when we get back. I believe that we'll find out that there aren't that many differences between us. I know who I am and what I do. It may seem crazy to you; but I also know that I love you, I want you to remember that. I may not have a chance to tell you that for a little while, until this gets straightened out. Promise me that you'll remember. Don't doubt that and don't doubt yourself. I'm not David. I won't let you down. I will be with you just as soon as and as much as I'm able to be once the circus of me being back and the movie shoot is over." He kissed her softly with more promise than passion.

Maggie's arms circled around him and kissed him back.

Maggie examined his face looking for some falsehood, but found none. She sighed. "I promise. I love you, too, although I probably shouldn't, and I know exactly who and what you are. I know things are going to be nuts for a while. I will try to remember that you will come to me when you're able to. You know how to reach me. I'll be here."

They went back into the house to wait. It wasn't long until they heard the sounds of heavy engines coming up the drive. They held each other and kissed passionately one last time, then opened the door. A snowplow was coming up the drive, followed by a state police car. As soon as they got up to the cabin, two troopers got out and walked up to them.

"Mornin'. Would you be Maggie Jones?" the taller of the two troopers asked.

"Yes. I got stuck here when the storm hit last Friday. That pine blew over and completely destroyed my truck. I had no way of calling for help."

"We got that report from your coworkers. You two okay?"

"I am but he—"

Ty interrupted her. "My name's Tyler Sinclair. Maggie found me in the woods shortly after she arrived. I'd been carjacked and thrown out of the car near here."

The trooper looked at Ty spotting his injuries, and went back to the cruiser. When he returned he had some papers in his hand. "We had a report about you being missing. Your car was found in Latrobe four days ago. We'll need to get a statement from both of you."

"No problem. Right now, though, he needs to be checked at the hospital. He's had a concussion and a few cracked ribs." Maggie became assertive, a nurse again, for her patient. In only a few minutes, Maggie's bag was in the trunk of the cruiser and she, Ty, and Taser were in the back seat.

The troopers gave them the use of their cell phones. Maggie called the hospital to let them know she was safe, and on her way, then she alerted them that the troopers were also bringing someone else, who had been stranded by the storm, who needed to be checked over. Ty gave her a strange look as he heard what she had said on the phone.

"I wasn't sure you wanted anyone to know what happened to you or who you are until you talk to Mike."

"Good thinking. Maybe you're right."

Ty called Mike and told him what had happened and to meet them at the hospital. The troopers let Maggie drop Taser off at her house, then took them to the hospital. Maggie was glad it was still early in the morning, the Emergency Department wasn't too busy yet; maybe Ty could get in and out without anyone recognizing him, she could only hope.

While Ty was in triage, Maggie changed into scrubs to begin her workday, and got report on the other patients in the E.D. She was aware of the looks she was getting from the others, but she wasn't in the mood to explain. Other than to thank them for sending help and telling them about the storm and her truck being smashed, she didn't mention that Ty had spent the week with her. Despite the promises she and Ty made to each other at the lodge, she was not sure they could keep them. She wanted to keep those memories to herself and not share them with anyone. The troopers had left before she was back in the main E.D. promising to be back for their statements.

Dr. Samuels came over to her to see how she was. "I heard your truck got smashed and you spent the week in your lodge. You okay, Maggie, any other damage done?"

"Not too much, the corner of the porch was hit, but the truck took the brunt of it. I'm all right. I wasn't near the truck when it was hit." Maggie hesitated, then said, "Allen, what about Ty, is he all right?"

"My hunch was right, you do know who he is. He isn't just someone the troopers randomly found in the woods near the cabin on their way to get you, is he; you found him? I figured as much when I saw the gash on his head, and how it had been bandaged. He's fine, you did good, kiddo. You want to talk about it?"

She smiled at Allen. "No, I don't want to talk about it right now…maybe later?"

Allen put his arm around Maggie. "When you need to talk to someone I'll be around." He gave Maggie a short hug. "I'm glad you're in one piece. I was worried when you didn't show up this morning. That's why I sent out the search party."

"I know, Allen, and I appreciate that. Right now I just need to…." Maggie didn't get to finish because of loud voices coming from the registration desk.

"I don't care what you say, I'm going back there and see what's going on! What are you people running here? He called me telling me he was being brought to this hospital, now where is he?!"

Maggie went out to the registration desk and came face to face with a middle-aged, slightly balding man, dressed in a three-piece suit in need of a good pressing. His face was flushed with a few days growth of faintly gray stubble. She could see the veins in his forehead and neck bulge as he continued his tirade. She moved toward him, trying to think how to calm him down.

"You must be Mr. Andrews. I'm Maggie Jones, the triage nurse. Please tell me how I can help you."

"Well, missy, you can start by telling me what in the hell is going on here! I got a call to meet my friend here, and no one seems to know anything about him! What kind of place are you running?"

Mike Andrews' face was becoming redder by the minute. Maggie actually thought he might burst any second.

"I can understand your frustration, Mr. Andrews. Come with me, and let's get this sorted out." She led him into one of the exam rooms, closed the door, and turned to face him, her voice hard. "First, sit down and calm down. Second, I recognized Tyler Sinclair. He told me what had happened; and didn't want information about him released, until after he spoke to you. I respected his wishes. Since he had evidence of a concussion, I registered him as a John Doe, to give him some privacy for now. Third, you need to get yourself under control, so I can take you back to see Mr. Sinclair, or I will have Security remove you."

Mike sat staring at her for a few seconds, then started laughing. "I like your spirit, missy. I would apologize, but it's against my nature. Suffice it to say, I wasn't thinking about anything but Ty's condition, and the fact that his car was found four days ago with no sign of him. I've been worried sick. I will say thank you, though, for not using his real name; that was good thinking. I believe I've calmed enough to see him if you would be so good as to take me to him."

Maggie opened the door and escorted Mike to the cubicle where Ty was waiting. Mike came in.

"Well, you don't look too bad considering the storm. They took care of you by the looks of it."

Maggie turned to leave but Ty reached for her hand.

"Mike, this is Maggie. She saved my life."

"I've met her, she gave me what for, when I became a little too loud, demanding answers. As for saving your life, isn't that what nurses are supposed to do?" Mike asked hostilely. He didn't like the way Ty was holding Maggie's hand, or how he was looking at her.

"Mike, shut up and listen. She found me last week during the storm. I've been with her since then. She took care of me."

"Well, well, well. So, when you told me you recognized Ty and had him registered as John Doe, that was for your benefit as well, then? Buys you a little more time, for the tabloids to start a bidding war, for your story of how you spent a week snowbound in a cabin with Ty Sinclair? I wonder how much that story will be worth."

"What the hell are you talking about? What's all this about the tabloids?" Ty looked at Mike as if he'd lost his mind.

"You don't think she hasn't got an angle, do you? The tabloids would love a story like that. Nothing like a bidding war to get the most from a one-time deal. After all, she can make a mint selling this story to the tabloids: *Ty Sinclair in a blizzard in a love nest*. I've heard nurses don't make much, a little extra cash this time of year can come in handy. Or, maybe she's hoping for a payoff to keep silent then?"

Maggie pulled herself out of Ty's grasp and fought to remain calm. "Mr. Sinclair, Mr. Andrews, I think it's best if we discontinue this conversation. Dr. Samuels will be in to see you with some instructions for discharge. It was a pleasure meeting you, Mr. Sinclair; I enjoyed playing chess with you. I also look forward to seeing the movie when it's released. Mr. Andrews, I will try to overlook your comments about my character because of the stress of seeing your client in this condition. I will also assure you that I will not be on the Medic Team for the movie set during Mr. Sinclair's shooting schedule. I wouldn't want you to think I'm trying to cash in on our brief acquaintance. When you've been discharged, one of the orderlies will escort you to Mr. Andrews' car, Mr. Sinclair. Good luck with the movie." Maggie kept her head high as she walked out of the cubicle. She made it to the locker room before she erupted in a spate of furious tears.

Maggie sank onto a bench in front of the lockers. She was seething with the sleazy and sordid nature of Mike Andrews' comments about selling Ty's story to the tabloids. "He's obnoxious. How could he say those things! I would never sell what happened to the tabloids. It wouldn't be professional, not to mention that it was private. Like I would take money to not say anything about last week!" She sat there fuming and talking to herself about Mike, what he could do with his attitude, and his payoff! She valued her privacy too much to do anything like that; she also would not do that to Tyler. He had come to mean too much to her, and what had happened between them was a treasure for Maggie alone.

Maggie heard the door to the locker room open she, hurriedly wiped the angry tears away. The last thing she needed was to have one of the other nurses become aware of the events of the last week. Maggie heard the steps behind her and felt an arm wrap around her. She twisted on the bench and felt Ty's lips on hers. He wiped the tears from her face, and held her close. She wrapped her arms around his neck and she instantly responded to his touch.

"Dr. Samuels told me you'd be in here. Maggie, don't pay attention to Mike. He's only trying to look out for me. He's been my friend forever, as well as my agent and manager. He thinks everyone has an angle. He's been around too many people who play to the tabloids, he's not used to people who do things without an ulterior motive."

"I'm sorry I reacted like that. It just rubbed me the wrong way; he practically accused me of keeping quiet about who you were, when the police brought us here, just so I could make money from the experience! That is just too crude for words! I'm not going to say anything to anyone about the lodge, not just for you, but for me as well. What happened there was wonderful, and was only for us, not the tabloids. It's a memory that I'll treasure and cherish forever."

"I know that, honey. Mike doesn't know you, but he will come around as soon as he knows what kind of person you are and that I love you."

Maggie smiled up at him. "You'd better go. Mike will be wondering what you're still doing here. Talk to you later."

He pulled her to him and kissed her thoroughly. With that, he left the locker room, Maggie was left staring at the door, dazedly. She touched her lips, smiled to herself as she too left the locker room, and went back to the nurses' station.

She had just finished giving discharge instructions to a patient, when an ambulance arrived with a ten-year-old boy who had fallen from a second-floor window. She helped the medics get the boy settled and started to assess his condition. She knew the neurosurgeon on call had been notified and would be down soon; she wanted to have a complete assessment finished before he arrived. As she finished, she heard the curtain swish open and looked up to see David Willis. She didn't know he was on call today, just what she needed after the morning she'd had. She took a deep breath, and began to give David report on the little boy.

"Dr. Willis, this is Charles Lowe. He's ten and fell from a second-floor window about thirty minutes ago. He was conscious at the scene, but has since lost consciousness; medics placed a collar and backboard on him prior to transporting him here. His pupils are unequal: the right is four millimeters and reacts briskly, the left is two millimeters and sluggish. He reacts to pain only. Pulse is 86 but regular, respirations are 30 and shallow, and BP is 90/50. Clear drainage noted from left ear and left nares. CT is ready when you are. The medics started an eighteen gage IV in his antecubital vein and I've sent labs and a type and cross. Lactated Ringers is infusing at keep open rate."

David nodded, and the two of them moved Charles to the CT scanner. While they waited for the test to be completed, Maggie called the operating room, placing them on standby, for a possible craniotomy as soon as the scan was completed. Once the scan had confirmed that Charles did have a head injury, and would require surgery, he was moved back to the E.D. cubicle so that his family could see him before he went into the operating suite. Maggie comforted a visibly and vocally distraught mother, while the child's father remained quiet with tears streaming down his face.

"I had been out of town last week. I got home and decided I needed to get the house secured for winter after that freak storm, so I took the storm windows up to the bedrooms. I got the screens out and I turned my back for just a moment, to move the screens out of the way, when I heard Charlie. I looked behind me, there he was, leaning out the window, I shouted at him to get away from there. I must have scared him, he started, and then I saw him falling out the window. I couldn't get to him." Mr. Lowe sobbed and slid down onto the chair.

Mrs. Lowe moved out of Maggie's arms to sit beside her husband wrapping her arms around him. "Chuck, it isn't your fault. It was an accident. The doctors will fix him." She looked up at Maggie, willing her to agree with her.

"Mr. and Mrs. Lowe, we will do everything we can to get Charlie through this. Come; give him a kiss so we can take him to surgery." Maggie reached down to the anguished parents and led them to Charlie's still figure.

They both leaned over and kissed him gently, telling him that they loved him and would be right here when he woke up. They accompanied him up to the surgical suite where they were directed to the waiting room.

Maggie returned to the E.D. and restocked the cubicle. It was nearly eleven-thirty. She was looking forward to going home and relaxing; it had been a long day. Maggie finished her shift and dragged herself home. Tomorrow she would have to look for a new vehicle. That would be after she talked to the police and the insurance agency. Right now, all she wanted was a hot shower and then bed; it had been a long day. She took that back it had been a long *eight* days.

Taser met her at the door when she came in, acting as if she'd been gone for years instead of only a few hours. He was beside himself with joy, with his tail wagging so rapidly she could hardly see it but heard the staccato beat as it hit the wall. Maggie took off her coat and went into the kitchen with Taser trotting behind her. She poured kibble and water to Taser's bowls. While Taser wolfed down the kibble, she went upstairs to shower and change.

The hot water relaxed muscles that Maggie wasn't even aware of being in knots. She stayed under the pulsating water until it became cold, thinking about the last eight days, smiling to herself when she thought of the last two nights at the cabin with Ty. She toweled dry and had begun blow-dry her hair, when the phone rang. She debated answering it, but gave in, sighing, and walked to the bedroom, picking up the receiver.

"Hello?"

"Hi, honey. Miss me yet?"

Maggie felt the smile start on her face, her heart skipping several beats. She admitted to herself why she had been so restless when she came home, and why her muscles had been so tense. Now hearing Ty's voice, she felt lighter and suddenly boneless.

"Who is this?" The happiness she was trying to hold back came through, she giggled as she said this.

"Well, that certainly deflates an ego. Here I thought I'd made an impression on you. I've missed you." The last part sounded wistful and Maggie's heart bubbled with joy at his admission.

"Ty, I am so glad you called. I have been thinking about you since you left the hospital. Is everything all right with Michael? How are you feeling?" Maggie sank down onto the bed and rubbed her damp hair with the towel as she waited for Ty's answer.

"I told Michael to mind his own business. You were not and are not a threat to my career, my privacy, or me. I feel fine; you did a good job patching me up. Even your doctor friend said so. He also told me that you were a good friend and didn't want to see you get used or hurt by someone with my reputation. I suppose I should expect that since he figured out that you patched me up in the first place."

Maggie found herself sputtering, "He did WHAT? Of all the unmitigated gall! Who does he think he is? I'll kill him!"

"Maggie, it's okay. I understand where he's coming from. Actors in general don't have a good rep for relationships; you've seen the tabloids. I want us to have one by the way. A relationship I mean, not a tabloid. Meet me tomorrow after you get off work? I'm staying at the Westin. We can go out for dinner, or stay in and order room service. I just want to spend some time with you in the real world, as you call it. I want to show you that I'm not going to dump you because I'm back in my world."

As much as Maggie wanted to spend time with Ty, she wasn't sure she was ready to jump into his world. "Is that a good idea? I mean, what about the paparazzi that have been hanging around, since you got back? I heard all about them camping out awaiting word about your disappearance. I don't think I'm ready for all that, not that they would know who I am but I would still have to navigate through them. Would you be upset if I asked you to come here? I'll make dinner and we can talk. I'm working the split shift, eleven A.M. to seven-thirty P.M." She trailed off and heard Ty's voice ask, "You're inviting me to your home?"

"Well, yes, but only if you want. Please, don't feel that you need to come. I only thought it would be better for you not to be seen at your hotel with some mystery woman for the tabloids to notice. Besides, as I said, I'm not anxious to meet the paparazzi." She waited to hear his answer, but was met with silence. "Nevermind, it was a bad idea." She scarcely realized that she had been holding her breath until, at the sound of Ty's chuckle, she let out the breath she had neglected to exhale.

"Yes, I would love to come to your place for dinner. Where and when?"

"615 Crafton Avenue, the house with the turret. If you get there before me, park in the drive. You can let yourself in; there's a rock by the back porch with *Taser's paws* engraved on it, the key is under the rock, and the security code is seven-nine-zero-five-one." As Maggie realized she was babbling, she held her breath, waiting to detect his reaction to her invitation.

"Maggie, you misunderstand me. I am surprised you trust me to be in your home when you're not there. You talk about valuing your privacy, and yet you invite me to take the key to your door and walk about your house without you being there." He wished he could see her eyes to determine how she was feeling about this conversation.

"Taser will be there to see you behave yourself, sir!" Maggie laughed at him. "Besides, you've been privy to some of very private areas; I hardly think having access to my home will be any more enlightening."

Ty heard her laughter and knew things would be all right with them. "Then I will be delighted to come for dinner. I'll see you at your house tomorrow evening. Now tell me what you're wearing." Maggie could picture his eyebrows wiggling as he flirted with her.

"Hmmmm. Right now, all I have on is a towel. You interrupted my shower." She was surprised at her brazenness in telling him she was practically naked, even if it was only over the phone. She heard his sharp intake of breath. "Woman, you are killing me! Of course, you can make up for it by wearing that for me tomorrow after dinner."

"I'll think about that. Maybe you could wear a matching one for me?" Who *was* this woman! She could not imagine talking to David in this manner even on the phone. She was beginning to think that maybe Ty was right; that the problem had been with David not with her.

"Earth to Maggie. Where did you go? I asked if you had any blue towels that match my eyes."

"I think I have just the thing. Hey, Ty?"

"What, sweetheart?"

"I think I am missing you. And not just the sex, either, although it was awesome but because I had a really good time with you, despite being stranded in a blizzard."

Ty's expression softened as she admitted this. He knew how he felt about her; for Maggie to admit that she missed him was a big step. She had to quit thinking of herself as a non-entity and value herself as much as he did. He knew she was afraid of entering into this relationship, not only because of what he did, but because she attributed his feelings as a sort of survivor syndrome, gratitude and closeness based on her helping him. He had to convince her that what he felt was real. "Maggie, thank you for that. I know it's difficult for you to open up. I'm not going anywhere and I won't hurt you. I love you. I hope someday you'll come to feel the same way about me."

"Ty…."

He could feel the emotion in her voice and thought she was just going to hang up but she continued after some minutes.

"I do trust you; I've invited you here, haven't I? Just don't push. I think it will take me some time to get used to you, so let's just go slowly."

"That's easy enough. But I would like there to *be* an us out of you and me. I'll give you the space you seem to need, so that I don't blow this chance with you."

They talked for a while, and eventually said goodnight. Maggie spun around her room with Taser barking and dancing around her.

"Taser, he says he loves me, can I believe him? I certainly hope so, because what I haven't told him is that I am *hopelessly* in love with him!" Maggie wasn't a bit sleepy now, even if it was a little after one in the morning.

She decided to call Tammy, her best friend since first grade. Tammy was a sexual assault detective who worked some strange hours, so Maggie wasn't afraid she would wake her. The phone went to voice mail, so Maggie left a long message telling her what had happened the last several days and her need to talk to her. She wanted to share this feeling of floating exhilaration she was experiencing, she wanted Tammy to tell her to grab onto it with both hands and enjoy the ride for as long as it lasted. Maggie had no illusions that despite what Ty said, this was not a forever kind of thing. There was some small part of her, locked deep inside her heart, that hoped she was wrong.

Ty, meanwhile, leaned against the bed's headboard and thought about the woman who had the power to make him laugh one minute and go crazy with her stubbornness the next, and in between make him weak with wanting her soft and pliant under him. He loved her humor, slightly warped as it was, she said it was a way of coping with some of the horror she saw on her job at times. She was immensely passionate, but didn't seem to realize it. How could she not realize what she did to him? He remembered the feel of her heat surrounding him, as she wrapped herself around him, drawing him deeper inside her. He could hear her soft mewls of pleasure begin deep in her throat and erupt with his name on her lips as she exploded under him. Thinking about her made his sex throb with desire.

Ty walked to the shower and turned the water on cold, he stood under it until he felt more in control. As he toweled dry he cursed the unknown David for making his Maggie feel wanting. *His* Maggie? He could only hope he knew how to take it slowly with her and prayed that his self-control would hold out that long. He closed his eyes and could see her lopsided smile as they played in the snow with Taser. The wind whipped her hair around her face and her cheeks were pink from the cold. It was her eyes that really held him though. Deep, brown with golden flecks, and sparkling with laughter. She told him she had never had a better day than this one with him, and impulsively kissed him. That was the moment he became lost in those eyes, and wanted to do whatever it took to keep that expression in them. Tomorrow night he'd see her again. He felt like a child waiting on Christmas Eve, too excited to sleep, but knowing that the sooner he did, the faster Christmas would come. He forced himself to relax, and thought some TV might make him sleepy. Instead, the first thing he saw was the news story about his having been reported missing for eight days, and his reappearance today at West Park General Hospital, with some broken bones. No mention of where he was found, for which Ty was grateful; Maggie wouldn't be hounded by the press then.

Then another thought hit him, his parents! Damn, he needed to call them, instead of just seeing the story on the news, they should hear the story first hand from him. He dialed the number and heard his mom's voice.

"Hello?"

"Mum, I just called to hear your voice, and to tell you that in spite of what the news may have said, I am all right."

"I imagined I would be hearing from you today. Since they didn't say you were dead, I wasn't too concerned." Ty heard the lie in her voice, as well as the attempt to cover it. He felt guilty for not calling his parents earlier. Ty filled his mother in on the events of the past several days ending with "I'm not sure what is going on, the police are involved and are investigating. I didn't see very much, so I can't give them much to use. I *am* okay, nothing major in the way of injuries. I want to talk about something else, though." Ty hesitated; did he really want to talk about Maggie to his mother? If he did, she would start planning a summer wedding and Ty wasn't all that sure Maggie felt the same about him.

"Tyler? Are you still there? What's wrong?" His mother's voice was becoming strained with his silence, Ty knew he would tell her about this remarkable woman.

"Nothing's wrong. I met someone and I wanted to tell you about her." Ty told his mother how Maggie had rescued him and took care of him for those first few days, when he was confused and unsteady. He told her how she protected him by not revealing his identity to anyone at the hospital, and how she stood up to Michael when he challenged her integrity.

"Mom, she's beautiful. She has the most glorious red hair that shimmers with gold in firelight. We played in the snow with her dog and she just glows when she's happy. Her dog is crazy, though, he kept trying to catch snowballs in his mouth. He looked so baffled when they disintegrated as he bit them. She puts chocolate chips in her pancakes! Can you imagine that? And, she plays chess, really well, too." Ty recognized that he was babbling but he didn't care; he wanted his mother to see Maggie through his eyes and realize she was special to him. He told her about Maggie's theory that he was drawn to her, only because they shared that time at the lodge, and he was grateful to her. When Ty finished he held his breath waiting for his mother to say something.

"Tyler, do you believe that you are attracted to Maggie because she helped you when you needed help?"

"No, Mum, I feel as if I've been looking for her forever; she makes me feel peaceful and, I don't know…whole somehow. It has nothing to do with gratitude. I'm sure of that."

"I think that means you have feelings for this girl. If you feel as strongly about her as it sounds, then by all means, keep her close. Honey, what does your heart tell you to do? When do we get to meet her?"

This was the part that Ty was dreading, having his family meet Maggie before she was ready to commit to a relationship with him. He explained this to his mother about how David had hurt her, and how she wanted to move slowly, to get to know him better. His mother agreed that it was a good idea, especially because Maggie felt they were too different to make a lasting relationship work. Ty and his mother made tentative plans for his parents to visit after the holidays and meet Maggie, as long as they didn't make a production of it. He then talked about things at home before Ty told his mother he loved them all and broke the connection.

His mother ended the call by saying, "It will all be straightened out; let the police do their job and you and Maggie continue to do yours."

Maggie was watching the same story and was glad she hadn't been mentioned, but wondered how the story got out; probably Michael, doing damage control. She knew he was just doing his job by protecting Ty, but she didn't like how he jumped to conclusions about her integrity. The phone rang, and expecting Tammy's call, she grabbed it during the first ring.

"Hello?"

It wasn't Tammy's voice that answered her. "You need to stay away from him. You'll be destroyed if you don't. You've been warned."

She heard the click as the connection was broken. The voice was strange and distorted almost robotic in tone. She looked at the caller ID only to read that it was a blocked number. The phone rang again; this time she waited until the caller ID showed Tammy's number before answering.

"Tammy! Did you just call me?"

"Hello to you, too. No, Nate and I just got in. What's wrong? You sound upset."

Maggie told her about the last eight days, finding the tire tracks near the lodge turnoff, and Taser finding Ty. She ended with the phone call just a few minutes ago. "Ty thought it was just a random carjacking, but now, after the call, I'm not so sure. What do you think?"

"I think you're letting your imagination run away with you. You watch too many true crime stories. If it will make you feel any better, I'll look into it. I'll meet you at the Major Crimes Bureau in the morning for your interview if you'd like. Okay?"

"Yeah, thanks. You think I went off the deep end huh?"

"Maybe a little. Now tell me all about the hunk. I hear it in your voice that he's something special. I know you have a crush on him, since you drag me to every movie he's in."

They spent the next half hour talking about Ty; how Maggie thought she could be falling for him. She hoped that Tammy would talk her out of it, but instead, she told Maggie to go for it and enjoy being with someone who made her feel good. They said goodbye and hung up. Maggie was still a little jumpy about the anonymous phone call but decided that she couldn't do anything about it now and all but convinced herself it was a wrong number. She finally fell asleep and began dreaming.

Maggie was leaving work, excited about seeing Ty again. As she walked toward the hospital garage, she thought she heard footsteps behind her. She was glad she had found a space on the hospital level, so she didn't have to use the elevator or steps. As she neared the truck, she clicked the remote starter and heard the engine roar to life. She was almost to the truck, when a hand grabbed her from behind. A voice whispered into her ear, "Stay away from him or you'll be sorry; she won't be warned again." She felt the tip of a knife at her throat pinch her, then she was thrown against her truck. By the time she was able to turn around, there was no one in sight.

Maggie woke with a start, her heart pounding in her chest, sweat pouring off her face. The call must have spooked her more than she originally thought. She got up, and padded down to the kitchen for a drink of water, looking at the clock. It was almost six, she might as well get up and get ready for the meeting with the police.

CHAPTER 8

Maggie took Taser with her when she went for her walk around the track near her house. She kept telling herself that she was just being cautious, as she looked around her, when she walked down the steps of the back porch. It had nothing to do with the phone call from last night. Since there were only the usual walkers on the track, she relaxed and enjoyed the early morning; saying hello to the walkers she saw every day, many of whom fussed over Taser. After completing the four outer laps of the track that made up the mile, Maggie went back home to shower and make breakfast; and then leave for the meeting with the police. When Maggie arrived at the Major Crimes Bureau, she found Tammy waiting for her as promised. The two women entered the building together, and headed toward the detective's desk.

"Jacob Bowen is handling this investigation but he had no problem with me sitting in with you for moral support. You remember Jacob, don't you? My old partner? The big hulking type who shaves his head?"

Maggie vaguely remembered the big detective from a party at Nate and Tammy's. She had just sat in the chair by Detective Bowen's desk when she heard his chuckle behind her. "Like I always say, Tammy, God only made a few perfect heads, so I have to display mine! Hi Maggie, how are you? This is only a routine follow up since you found the victim. I just need a timeline of events."

Maggie went through the events of the past eight days. How she saw the tire tracks and footprints near the turn off for her lodge. She told them how Taser was the one who actually found Tyler in the snow. Jacob told her she would need to sign the statement when it was typed. Within an hour she left the police station, and went back home to phone the insurance company to report the damage to her truck and porch. She also arranged to rent a vehicle until she could get a new truck. The rental agency would drop the truck off at the emergency department sometime after lunch. By now, it was almost ten-thirty, her shift started at eleven. Maggie walked the ten blocks to the hospital, but kept looking around for anyone who seemed interested in her actions. *This is silly*, she thought, *no one is paying any attention to me. Forget that phone call, it was a wrong number and not meant for me.*

There were few patients in the emergency department when she arrived at a quarter to eleven. She, and one of the other nurses, began the monthly check of the resuscitation equipment until they needed to see patients. They checked the expiration dates of the emergency drugs and sterile packages. Once the exchange of outdated materials and drugs was completed, it was time to start lunch relief. David came into the E.D. to tell her that Charlie was doing better. He had regained consciousness during the night and seemed to have no ill effects from the fall. He would be in the hospital for a few more days and was grouching that he would miss Halloween. Maggie laughed and said she'd make a trick-or-treat bag for him. When David left, Maggie wasn't as upset as she usually was when she ran into him. She had Tyler to thank for that.

The car rental agency delivered her truck as promised. The afternoon and early evening passed quickly. There were several patients to be treated. Maggie split the time between triaging and treating patients in the cubicles. Most were seen then discharged, but one patient, who came in right after dinner, was admitted. Since he was Maggie's patient, she was late getting off work because she needed to transfer the patient to his room and give a report to the nursing staff. She hadn't thought about Ty since she left for work this morning, but now she wondered if he had indeed come to her house. Had he let himself in? Was he playing with Taser? She felt butterflies in her stomach with anticipation.

While Maggie was finishing her transfer and paperwork, Ty had taken a cursory look of the first floor while he waited for Maggie to come home. The dining room was so old-fashioned and formal, he doubted that Maggie used this room much. The table was dark walnut. The legs were carved with geometric shapes. The dry sink and china cabinet matched the table, with the addition of pineapples carved into the doors. To him it looked like something out of the Disney version of the Seven Dwarfs' home; he fully expected the furniture to break into song. He continued to move around her house, admiring the furniture. Most of it was antique and similar in design to that in the lodge. Maggie told him that it all belonged to her great-great-grandparents, who had built the lodge and house in the late 1890s.

He noted that some of the light fixtures were the original gaslight fixtures, they had been converted to electricity. The living-room walls were painted a soft caramel color, with a contrasting darker brown paper border around the ceiling and chair rail. The ceilings were at least twelve feet high. The bay window had a window seat padded in the same material as the sofa. He could easily picture Maggie curled up there reading. The floors were highly polished dark wood with area rugs, and big cushy pillows placed in front of the fireplace. There were photos of generations of her family on the mantle.

Tyler petted Taser's head, and looked around the kitchen. It was a pleasant room. The walls were a pale peach color with southwestern accents throughout the room. The center island was wood with a green granite top. The floor was well-worn red brick, with scatter rugs at the back door leading to the mudroom. Shutters at the windows were open to let in the light. The appliances were all modern and stainless steel. Ty guessed that Maggie used this room quite a bit since she had told him how she loved to cook and bake, especially for the holidays. He turned the oven on low, and placed the Chinese take-out he brought with him inside to keep warm, until Maggie got home. He tried to remember what Maggie had told him her favorites were. He had hot and sour soup, General Tso's chicken, crab Rangoon, eggrolls, and fried dumplings. Ty looked at the clock again and saw it was after eight; Maggie's shift ended a half hour ago.

"She's late, Taser. Do you think she regrets asking me to come? I hope not. She has come to mean a great deal to me. She's smart, inventive, funny, and passionate. Very passionate, and in more ways than one." Tyler grinned lasciviously to Taser. "How could that idiot man say she was frigid? She could set off smoke alarms with the heat that radiates from her."

Taser barked once, and Ty took it that the dog at least agreed with him.

The lights were on in the living room, but that was no way to tell if anyone was there, since the lights were on a timer; she didn't like to come home to a dark house. As she turned into the drive and opened the garage door, she noted that a car was in front of the second garage, and that the lights were on in the kitchen as well. She was giddy with happiness, barely able to contain herself, as she parked the car and sprinted up the back steps and into the mudroom.

"Tyler? Are you here? Taser? Where are you?"

She walked into the kitchen and came face to face with him. There he was sitting at the counter, drinking a glass of water and talking to Taser. Taser trotted over to nudging her hand with his nose, begging to be petted. Maggie knelt down, took his big head in her hands, and rubbed him behind his ears. She needed this time to make her heart slow down, and pray that the heat she felt wasn't visible on her face. Ty walked toward her, lifting her up for his embrace.

"Are you regretting your invitation?" There was concern in his voice.

"No. Oh, no, not at all. I'm very glad you're here. Let me change, then I'll fix dinner." She moved toward the door to the hall, when Ty's voice stopped her.

"I brought dinner for us. I remembered you talking about your favorite Chinese restaurant, and ordered for us. It's in the oven keeping warm. Maggie, look at me, please."

She turned slowly toward him and lifted her head to meet his eyes.

"What is wrong? I feel that you're pulling away and avoiding me."

"I'm not avoiding you. Well, maybe a little bit. Now that you are here, I *am* feeling a little overwhelmed. I'm not sure how to act with you here. In my house, I mean. Back to reality. The lodge was sort of unreal, if you know what I mean."

Ty strode over to her, and lifted her chin to look into her eyes.

"I talked to my mother last night about you. I know you think that this is only reaction to you rescuing me and that this isn't real. I think it is, and I want to give it a chance. I asked Taser if he agrees with me, and he does."

She searched his face looking for some way to know if he meant what he had said. "I've heard that relationships that start because of a crisis or stress never last. It's the heat of the moment and the adrenalin rush that makes them think it's love when it's just relief that they survived combined with lust."

"Go and change your clothes. I'll get the stuff out of the oven and then we'll talk." He kissed the tip of her nose, and turned back to the oven; she sighed and went upstairs.

When she came back down in sweats and a T-shirt, Ty had set the island with bowls of Chinese food and lit candles. He came and pulled out the chair for her, kissing the back of her neck as he pushed the chair under the countertop.

They ate in relative silence, neither wanting to bring up the subject they broached before she went to change. They were playing with chopsticks, trying to eat and not miss their mouths, laughing when they managed to get food into the right place. Ty fed pieces of beef to Taser who was sitting under his chair while Maggie pretended she didn't see. When they couldn't eat any more, they cleared the table and washed the dishes. Ty took her hand, and led her into the living room. He sat on the sofa and pulled her onto his lap. He was content to sit there with her; would be content to sit there forever. She made him comfortable and brought a peace into his life. He never thought about what he did before; he was happy being an actor, but thinking about the people he met none, of them were quite real. They all wanted something from him. Maggie was a giver, she gave him part of herself, not just as a lover, but also, as a person, a friend. Lord knows he didn't have many people in his life he could call friend. After the initial shock of who he was had worn off, he got the feeling that she treated him as she would any one of her friends. She didn't treat him as someone special because of who he was. She wasn't embarrassed because of the simplicity of the lodge, or lack of electricity, or what food she fixed for them. He saw what she was inside, and when he loved her, she glowed making his world light up as never before. He needed to make her see all this. She was his, and he didn't intend to let her get away.

"Maggie, I know you're worried that this isn't real. We did meet under unusual circumstances, but you've brought so much to my life that I didn't know was missing before. I want the kind of life my parents have, the same kind of love and togetherness. I want you with me always. I hadn't planned on saying anything, because I thought you might think it was too soon to tell you how I feel. But I swear to you, I mean every word I say." Ty reached out for her hand and brought it to his lips.

"Ty, I know you think you love me. No, wait—hear me out," she said as he tried to interrupt her. "All I'm asking is that we take this slowly. Give ourselves time to know each other in the real world, and not in a snowbound lodge. We can see each other, and talk to each other and whatever else happens, happens." She took his hand and kissed his palm, closing his fingers over the spot she had touched with her lips.

Tyler thought over what she had said. Initially, he wanted to dismiss her concerns, but the more he mulled over her words, the more they made sense; making him realize that he did have to take things slowly for Maggie's sake. He believed that what they had was real, but he also realized that Maggie needed to be convinced that his feelings were genuine, and if she wanted to move slowly, then that was what he would do even if it killed him to do so.

He nodded and agreed to take things slowly. "Does that mean that all we do is talk when we see each other, and am I supposed to keep my hands to myself?"

Maggie laughed. "No, I said that whatever happens between us happens. Just so I don't bruise your ego entirely, I enjoyed making love with you. And, to risk making your ego even bigger than it already is, you're my first orgasm. I don't believe I said that." Maggie could feel the heat rushing to her face as she covered it with her hands and felt like all kinds of fool.

"Why are you embarrassed about that? I will let my ego inflate with that." Ty grinned and winked at her. "Besides, David was wrong; you are far from frigid. You could have set the lodge on fire with your passion. Did you ever stop to think that maybe it was him that was a rotten lover, not you?"

Maggie could only stare at Tyler. She had never thought about the possibility that David could be at fault. He had been her first lover, but she had thought David loved her. Tyler had given her quite a bit to think about. David had been new to the area and she *was* one of the first people he met. He must have asked her out just to be nice, sort of payment for her help. Maybe it was his fault that she didn't get the hang of making love with him, maybe she only thought she loved him. What she felt for Tyler was so much stronger. He said she was passionate and hot, he wasn't complaining about their lovemaking, so maybe she was able to do it right.

Tyler thought he should change the subject. He didn't want her to think that he had only one thought in his head, even if it was true. "I looked through your collection of DVDs; why don't we watch a movie and make out on the couch?"

"Why don't you pick it out and I'll make popcorn?" Maggie headed toward the kitchen as Ty rummaged through the DVD cabinet.

They munched popcorn cuddled on the sofa watching *Casablanca* and reciting the dialogue along with the characters. The phone rang and Maggie jumped at the sound. She really didn't want to answer it, but, also didn't want him to know she was frightened. She got up and picked up the receiver.

"Hello?"

The robot voice from the night before answered her, "You ignored my warning. You were with him again. I saw you and I know you talked to the police. I know everything you do. You can't hide from me. Stay away from him or you will be hurt."

Click, and the phone went dead.

Maggie's hands were shaking as she replaced the receiver; she knew that the calls were meant for her, mention of the *police* confirmed it. She wasn't aware that Tyler had been watching her. When he saw the color drain out of her face, he rushed over to her. She looked at him without really seeing him.

"Maggie, who was that on the phone? What's wrong?"

Ty took her hand, and was shocked to feel how cold it was. She was still pale and shaking as he led her back to the sofa. He knelt in front of her and kept her hands in his.

"Maggie, c'mon, honey. What's wrong? Who was that, what did they want?" Maggie's eyes were still unfocused and Tyler was beginning to get scared. What was going on? What was that phone call about that frightened her so much that she was almost in shock? He moved up beside her and took her in his arms. He held her tight, as he felt her tremble, and felt her heart beating too fast. He rubbed his hands up and down her back and kissed her temple. After what seemed an eternity, he felt her relax, the shaking stopped and her breathing became more regular. She made no effort to move away from him, so he stayed right where he was, holding on to her and kissing her. She moved slightly, but only to raise her face to his, and returned his kiss. She put her arms around his neck and held on for dear life.

"Maggie, what was that phone call about?" Ty's voice was a mere breath beside her ear. In his arms she felt safe, and then realized she had been acting like a crazy woman. She started to pull away from his arms but he refused to let her go. "No, darlin', stay right here and tell me what's going on. Tell me what I can do to help."

She took a deep breath, and told him about the call last night and then just now. She held on tighter to him as she told him how weird the voice was. "But I don't know what the voice means about minding my own business or to stay away from you. Why would he say that? Maybe it means that your kidnapping was not a random act but that you *were* the target. How does he know my involvement with your rescue? I'm going to call Tammy and tell her I received another one of those calls. Maybe she'll have some ideas."

Maggie told Tammy about the new call, and what the robotic voice said.

"Until I can get someone there to trace the calls, just screen the calls."

"Tammy, I don't think that will work, the caller I.D. is always blocked and he never stays on longer than to say one or two sentences."

"Then we'll just tape the calls and analyze them for background noise and voice recognition. I'll be over in the morning for now, try to relax."

After they discussed what time Tammy could bring a tech over in the morning, they hung up. Maggie still felt wound up and paced the room, closing the shutters and drapes. Taser sensed her mood and paced with her, his big head bumping her hand at intervals so that she absently scratched behind his ears.

Eventually, she settled on the sofa and looked up at him. "Am I being silly about this? Maybe I am overreacting. It unnerved me. That voice was just downright scary. Someone knows I was the one who found you. Why would they warn me to stay away from you?" Tyler opened his arms to pull her close and she moved into them and snuggled close. Her fingers made circles on the front of his shirt and soon he could feel the tension leave her body.

"I know we agreed to take it slow, honey, and I'm not pushing, but I don't think you should be alone tonight. I plan on staying here." He felt her stiffen for a moment, and then she pulled away and met his eyes. She nodded and answered, "I'm glad you suggested it. The guest room or…my room?" She gave him a faint smile but her eyes were still troubled.

"I get a choice?" He leered at her and wiggled his eyebrows, which made Maggie giggle. "What do you think, woman? How can I possibly pass up the chance to keep you close? Now that sleeping arrangements are settled, how about we watch the end of this movie, and cuddle some more? Let's try to get you un-wound, or you won't be able to sleep tonight."

With Taser curled on the floor, and Maggie snuggled up against him, they semi-watched the end of the movie sneaking in kisses and hugs. Tyler went around the house with her making sure all the doors, windows, and shutters were locked. Maggie set the alarm and together they went up the stairs to her room. The room was large, the floor looked like a quilt made of different shades and shapes of wood, which should look awful, but was somehow right in this room. One wall was floor-to-ceiling windows, just like in the lodge, with shutters over the bottom half and sheer pale blue curtains covering the top half. The other three walls were a pale blue that matched the curtains. The ceiling was white with a geometric pattern in the plaster, two ceiling fans rotated at each end of the room. There were two doors at the short end of the room, one of which led to the rooms' en-suite bath. An antique vanity and dresser were against the wall next to the second door. It was the bed however, that held his attention. It was a huge antique sleigh bed, similar to the one at the lodge, with a dark blue comforter, and pillows in the same shade of blue and a cedar chest at the foot of the bed. It wasn't what Ty had expected, although he wasn't sure what he did expect. Each time he thought he had Maggie pegged, she surprised him. Being stranded in a snowstorm with a wounded stranger and no means of communication or transportation didn't seem to faze her, but threatening anonymous phone calls threw her.

Tyler felt the tension radiating from Maggie. Was it left over from the phone call or because he was here in her room? She looked so lost and defeated as she moved about the room, gathering the clothes he recognized from the lodge that she usually slept in. She turned toward the bathroom door, tried to smile at him, but he could see the tears shimmering in her eyes. Seeing her like this broke his heart, and he moved toward her to gather her in his arms. She clung to him the way she had after the phone call. He could feel her slight trembling and lifted her chin to look into her deep whiskey eyes.

"I'm sorry, really. This isn't like me at all. I'm not the damsel-in-distress kind of woman." She seemed to shake herself mentally, and tried to grin at him but it looked more like a grimace. "I'm just so jittery and stressed; I think I need a hot shower to relax. I won't be long." She went into the bath and closed the door behind her.

He waited until he heard the water in the shower come on, then Tyler picked up the phone and hit redial to call Tammy. When she answered, he told her who he was and that Maggie was badly frightened about the phone calls, he was worried about her; worried enough to spend the night with her. He wanted to know if this was a good idea, or should he stay away from her to keep her safe, since the calls had warned against seeing him. Tammy was concerned, but didn't think that Ty should distance himself from her, at least not yet. Neither one could think why Maggie would be threatened, she didn't know anything about Ty's abduction; Ty was still having a hard time remembering what happened.

Tyler thought about letting Mike know where he was, but decided against it, he was still somewhat angry with him for thinking that Maggie would leak any information to the media.

Maggie came out of the bathroom in her sweats, her hair still damp and clinging to her cheek. He examined her face to evaluate her mood. Her eyes were clear and her trembling had stopped. She came up to him and wrapped her arms around his neck, reaching up to kiss him. She met his eyes and told him she was fine. "I'm calmer now." She grinned at him and gave him a gentle shove toward the bathroom. She curled up on the bed and opened the book she had been reading; willing herself to remain relaxed. She had the alarm system, and Taser was not going to let anyone get close to her if he didn't know them, or sensed her antipathy toward them. And, there was Tyler. She hated being weak and clingy, but she needed to have someone here with her tonight. Once she figured out what the caller wanted, she would be able to handle it. On that thought, Ty came out of the bathroom wrapped in a dark blue towel. She remembered what he had said last night when he called, and started to giggle.

"Seems I did have a towel that matches your eyes!"

"I should have thought to bring extra clothes with me but I wasn't planning a sleepover. Well, at least not on my first invitation to your house." Tyler leaned over and touched his lips to hers; he kept it light, not wanting to spook her. He wanted Maggie to come to him when she was ready, and he was prepared to wait.

Maggie shook her head at his silliness, and made room for him on the bed with open arms. He went willingly to her, gathering her close to his chest. Maggie's head rested on his shoulder, she sighed at how good this felt, and she relaxed completely. She curled up against him and leaned forward to kiss his neck, she could hear a low moan in his throat as his arms tightened around her, content to just hold her and keep her safe. He could feel Maggie's breathing slow, and knew she was asleep. He lay there staring at the darkness and thought about the events of the last several days. They were not all pleasant thoughts, who would want to get rid of him and why? His memory was beginning to return; he remembered that he hadn't been thrown from the car. When the car became stuck in the snow, the men got out, and attempted to push it free. Tyler saw his chance, and tried to make a run for it. One of the men fired at him and he fell, rolling down into the woods. He thought that's when he banged his head. Then nothing, until he woke up by the fire, with Maggie. He tried to remember details about the man who came up to his car as best as he could, but it was rather vague. He planned to tell Maggie about these memories in the morning, he didn't want to wake her knowing she was stressed enough.

He still didn't have any idea why someone would hurt him. Now, it seemed that because this small but strong woman dared to help him, she was at risk as well. He wouldn't, couldn't let anything happen to her. After trying to figure out who could be doing this, with no success, Tyler fell asleep.

CHAPTER 9

The light coming through the upper portion of the windows woke Tyler. Maggie was still asleep curled up against him, and he wondered how he was lucky enough to have found her, or rather, for her to have found him. The music of the alarm was starting to sound and Maggie reached sleepily behind her, groping for the snooze button. As soon as the music stilled, her eyes flew open and blood rushed to her cheeks giving her pale face color. She slowly met his gaze and tried to hide her embarrassment at being in bed with him.

"Good morning, sweetheart. Feeling better?" He kissed the top of her head, and slid his fingers under her chin to keep her gaze fixed on him, when she tried to burrow beneath the comforter.

"Um, good morning. I'm sorry I fell asleep before we…um, um," her voice trailed off in embarrassment. She could feel the heat flare in her face hotter than before; what an idiot I am, she thought.

"Before we made love? Is that what you're having trouble saying to me?"

"Yeah, I told you I'm not used to waking up with anyone, and then to invite you to stay the night, and then fall asleep on you, I mean…oh, hell!"

Tyler's chuckle startled her, this was not the reaction she had expected from him when she woke, and realized that they hadn't done anything. "If that was all I wanted from you, I wouldn't have stayed last night after you fell asleep." He grinned at her. "I knew you were stressed, and I was not going to take advantage of that. I told you, you mean more to me than a quick roll in the sack. So, what time do you have to be at work?"

Maggie glanced at the clock and jumped out of bed, saying she was going to be late for a staff meeting if she didn't hurry. She flew around the room, dragging scrubs out of the drawers and scurrying into the bathroom to get ready. Ty stayed where he was, grinning inanely at the bathroom door. Several minutes later Maggie emerged, dressed, her hair pulled back from her face and stopped to stare at him.

"I am acting like an idiot, right? It's okay, you can tell me." She began to laugh, and continued toward the door. "If you want breakfast, other than cereal, you'll have to make it for yourself. Coffee's ready, though, so come on down when you're dressed."

Tyler could hear her on the stairs, and Taser, after sparing a look in his direction, took off right behind her.

I could get very used to this, he thought, as he got out of bed and went to wash up for breakfast. When he walked into the kitchen, he found that Maggie had finished her cereal and was spreading peanut butter on toast. She was munching on half, and Taser was scarfing down his own slice.

Maggie thought that this was a nice way to start the day, and half-wished she didn't have to go to work, so she could spend the day watching Tyler. Tyler hesitated, then began to share the memories that had surfaced last night with her. "I'm still not sure who is behind this or why. I'm going to call Tammy and tell her what I remember."

"I think that's a good idea. Maybe she can have you work with a sketch artist and try to identify that man. I've got to get going, but make yourself at home, stay as long as you want."

She and Tyler compared their schedules for the day. Maggie would be home by six, but Ty's shooting schedule would keep him busy until the early morning. She suggested that he get some more sleep, but he told her that he wanted to talk to Tammy, and he needed to be on the movie set for today's shooting schedule. Then he planned to pack some clothes, so he could come back when filming was done for the day.

She looked surprised. "You're coming back tonight?"

"Would you rather I didn't come tonight? I thought, maybe, you might feel more comfortable if I stayed, until Tammy and the police find out more about your caller. Besides, it'll give me a chance to prove that I don't just want sex from you." He grinned, but held his breath waiting for her answer; he hoped she would want him to stay, but he reminded himself not to push, she was still wary of relationships. He silently rejoiced when he saw her face light up at his words.

"I would love to have you stay. For as long as you want." Maggie could feel herself blush again and cursed herself for not having more control over this. "Do you want…? I mean, are you asking…. Will you stay in my room?" She wanted the floor to open up and swallow her for her ridiculousness, and refused to meet his eyes. She heard him move toward her to sit in the chair next to her saying nothing until she did look up at him.

"Maggie, I want nothing more than to share your bed. You tell me if that's all right with you. If it is, then, that's where I'll be, and if not, the guest room is fine, too."

Maggie took a deep breath, all the while locking his gaze with hers. She seemed to make a decision and nodded. "I'd like you to stay with me, in *my* bed."

"I'm glad. Now go to work before you're late. I'll call you later." He helped her into her coat and watched as she pulled out of the garage and turned onto the street.

Tyler straightened the kitchen and then pulled out his cell phone. He had programmed Tammy's number into it last night, after he found it on Maggie's caller ID. He also made a mental note to call his family and let them know what was going on, before the tabloids had a chance to pick up that story as well.

Ty talked to Tammy for a long time explaining about what he now remembered of the abduction. When he finished the story, he waited for Tammy's comments.

"I'll see what I can find out. My first concern is Maggie, if those calls are because of you, then we'll have to consider other options. I know they spooked her more than she's letting on. I already called her and told her I'd bring a tech over this morning, to set up a trace on her phone. I can let myself in, if you won't be there; we have keys to each other's houses. I'd like you to work with a sketch artist, maybe it'll help jog your memory about what your gorilla friend looked like."

"Maggie said you might suggest that. Maggie told me to make myself at home until I needed to leave for the set, and I don't have to be there until one. Do you want to meet here, or should I come to the station?"

"I'll be there within the hour with the artist and a tech. You can work with the sketch artist while the tech works on Maggie's phone." Tammy hung up, and he sat in Maggie's bright kitchen, just thinking, for a long time.

Tammy arrived as promised, and the tech went to work on Maggie's phone. Tyler spent almost another hour with the artist, trying to pin down memories of the man who had pushed him into the car. By the time they were done, Ty was almost convinced that the artist had captured his abductor's likeness.

After Tammy left, Tyler pulled ingredients together for lasagna, so that Maggie would only have to put it in the oven to heat when she got home from her shift. He wanted to make things as easy for her as he could. Tyler still had no clue why anyone would want to kidnap him, or why someone would want to harm Maggie. He was still puzzling over this when he left for the movie set after lunch.

CHAPTER 10

"Cut! Tyler, what is wrong tonight? You aren't here at all. Let's take five, and get your head back on!" Sal's voice was strident with irritation, and Ty forcibly brought his mind back to the set and script.

"I'm sorry, Sal, you're right, I'm not concentrating." He wasn't going to explain what he was thinking about, but Sal had his own theories.

"Are you sure you don't need to take some time off? It was a harrowing experience being kidnapped, and stranded in a snowstorm. I'm sure you're still suffering the aftereffects of the concussion."

Although this was a good excuse, Tyler wasn't biting, and told Sal that he was fine, just a bit distracted. After that short break, they went back to work, and he made himself concentrate on the scene they were shooting. It was the scene where Kate delivers saws to Edward so he and Jack can break out of the jail. It was not a terribly difficult scene, but it was a pivotal one, as it set the tone for the attraction Kate had for Edward. Previous movies of this story made Kate attractive and seductive, but Sal was making Kate the way she was in reality. Ty felt sorry for Sara Buchanan, the actress playing Kate, because she was a truly beautiful woman. Sara said that she wanted this role to prove that she was more than a pretty face trying to be an actress, and she was getting her wish. They had worked together, several years ago, in a movie where she played the daughter of an English general stationed in India and he was the villain. It was difficult to see her as the somewhat disfigured Kate.

As he thought about that, he remembered Maggie saying she had every one of his movies on DVD, and had seen most of his plays, and always hated it when he played the villain, even if those were the better-defined roles because he usually died. Not even his parents could boast that fact. Maybe it was a sign that he meant more to her than she let on.

He shook his head to clear it. Better not to think of Maggie right now, he needed to concentrate. The sooner they got the scene completed, the sooner he could call her and hear her voice. The rest of the afternoon went without a hitch as Tyler kept his mind on the job, the cameras captured him and Kate during the escape scene. After several more takes from different angles, Sal was finally satisfied and called, "Lunch!"

The crew and cast headed toward the catering tent. The smells pouring out of the tent made his stomach growl. He picked up the plate set and headed toward the beef. He knew better than to get the chicken, after all, she had put the stuff in the chicken as he had directed. Many members of the crew were eating the chicken; boy were they going to regret it this afternoon.

He sat by himself, slowly chewing the roast. He should have grabbed bread and made a sandwich of it. Then he could have gone to the park and not watch the carnage that was about to happen. Ah, but where was the fun in that?

About twenty minutes after he sat down, one of the lighting techs lurched toward the port-o'-johns groaning as he went. Sounds of severe retching were heard near the front of the tent, and others began to have empathetic retching with him. Several got up and tried to run to the johns, but many wound up vomiting on the ground.

Tyler and Peter Bartmann, one of the assistant directors, were entering the tent just then and watched the scene before them.

"I think there's something wrong with the food," Peter whispered to Tyler.

"Ya think? We have to stop the line and find out what they ate. I'm going to call Maggie as well, since some of them might have to be seen. Give the hospital a heads-up."

Peter went to the beginning of the food line, while the assistant directors tended to the sick crewmembers, trying to find out what they had eaten. Ty called Maggie and alerted her to what was happening. She told him that she would have the E.D. ready and to get the set medics to bring them in.

As the medics drove the thirty-seven ill crewmembers to the hospital, Peter found out that they had all eaten the chicken and beef. He and Tyler picked a pan of each, and drove to the hospital with it as well. The crew all had the same symptoms, severe abdominal cramping pain, nausea, vomiting, and now diarrhea. Samples of all the fluids were sent for analysis, and the meat was sent to the pathology lab.

Maggie and the other nurses were busy starting intravenous lines and hanging fluids. They drew blood, changed bed linens, and assured the macho crewmembers that this was nothing to be embarrassed about, since food poisoning was a serious incident. Some of the crew responded to the fluids and admitted that they had only had one piece of either meat because they sampled all the choices available. Those that were sicker said that they only had the chicken to eat.

Ty wanted to talk to Maggie about the crew, but every time he was able to get close to her, someone called her to assist them. He watched her work, remembering how organized and tunnel-visioned she could be when she set herself to a task. She was amazing: efficient, friendly, and pointing out things that the nursing assistants could do to help make the crew comfortable without making it sound like she was issuing orders.

Ambulances came and went with other patients and Maggie set up a trauma room for an accident victim. David walked in just as the patient did, so he didn't have a chance to talk to Maggie, other than to ask if they could have coffee later.

"There's something I need to talk to you about."

Maggie looked at him as if he'd lost his mind, shook her head, and helped the medics move the female patient onto the bed. She avoided him as much as possible during the rest of the day but he found her in the break room and tried to talk to her.

"Look, David, I'm happy for you and Linda, but I really don't have anything to say to you, and I prefer it that way."

David grabbed her arm and Maggie shot him a look meant to wither him. He let her go and she took the cup of coffee with her as she went out the door.

The afternoon and evening passed quickly, and finally the initial results from the blood work and fluid specimens were back. There was no bacterial contamination in any of the samples. Now, they just had to wait for the chicken samples to provide an answer. By now, most of the crew were no longer vomiting, but were worn out, with sore muscles from the experience. Some had fallen asleep, and others were anxiously watching the nurses making rounds, checking vital signs and offering ice chips.

At midnight, the chicken analysis was back. Although there was no bacteria in any of the pieces, there was an anomaly. The chicken was full of Polyethylene Glycol: a strong powdered and tasteless laxative, sold over-the-counter as Miralax. The pathologist, Dr. Bircher, spoke at length to Peter, informing him that his was no accident. Someone had deliberately put it into the chicken. Since the chicken was made with a lemon dill sauce, and Miralax essentially had no taste, no one noticed the laxative in the chicken.

Ty now had the opportunity to talk to Maggie, she was finishing the necessary paperwork and getting ready to head home. He walked over to her cubicle and thanked her for helping with the problem. "Once again, you've come to my rescue. Even if I didn't eat any of the chicken, it was what I usually eat on set."

Maggie looked up at him. "Do you think this might have been meant for you? I admit it's a bit drastic to make most of the crew sick, but it also wouldn't look too obvious if you weren't the only one to become ill."

Tyler initially wanted to brush her worries aside, but considering that most of the crew had worked with him before, and knew his food choices during a shoot, he slowly nodded. "You might be on to something. Let's keep it to ourselves for now. Want some company tonight? I'm not quite ready to crash yet."

"That's another thing, why are you still here? You didn't eat any of the chicken and you weren't sick; so *why* did you come here?"

"I've worked with this crew before, movie sets are like a family. I was worried about them. Besides, it gave me a reason to watch you in action again." He grinned at her and she just shook her head at him.

"Go away for fifteen minutes so I can finish this paperwork. Then we can go home and relax." She didn't realize what she had said, but Ty picked up on it and smiled to himself. He was making headway with her.

CHAPTER 11

The next morning, Tyler returned to the movie set and found that only a few of the crew were missing. Peter called him and Sara Buchanan into the office trailer. When they arrived, Peter was already there with Sal, Mitch, the caterer, the other assistant directors, and the police waiting for them.

Jacob started by saying, "Dr. Bircher made it clear that this was no accident. The Polyethylene Glycol had to be deliberately put in the chicken. Mitch has worked with most of the catering staff before, but there are several new employees; some of whom are working as interns, for the experience and school requirements. We don't usually do background checks on them since we've dealt with the school before, and they do background checks on admission."

Detective Bowen stared at the list running the names through his memory for anyone with a police record. He came across one: Sandi Adams, she had a sheet for petty theft and shoplifting. This didn't sound like her kind of game, but he planned on questioning her anyway.

"Sandi Adams, was she working yesterday?" Detective Bowen looked at Mitch who examined the time sheet for yesterday.

"Yes, she came on at six-thirty and was finished at six-thirty, most of them work four twelve-hour days. Do you think she had something to do with it? I know she's had problems in the past, she told me about them, but she seemed to have cleaned up her act. She's a hard worker; always on time, never tries to mingle with the cast like some do."

"Let's just say that she's a person of interest. I'd like to talk to her. Can you have her come in here?" Although it appeared to be a question, Mitch viewed it as an order and went to get her. Several minutes later, he reentered the room with Sandi in tow.

"Ms. Adams, I'm Detective Jacob Bowen; I'd like to ask you a few questions. Please sit down."

Sandi glanced at the others assembled there and appeared nervous as she sat. "What kind of questions? I haven't done anything, I swear! Mitch, tell him…"

"Sandi, may I call you Sandi?"

Sandi nodded and Detective Bowen continued.

"I'm investigating the events of yesterday. I'll be questioning everyone involved with the preparation and serving of lunch."

Sandi still looked frightened, but nodded slowly. "Okay."

"Was there anything unusual about food delivery that you noticed?"

"No."

"What about anyone who didn't belong with the catering staff?"

"Some of the crew came by for coffee while we were preparing lunch, but that's not really unusual."

"Can you remember who came by?"

"Ummm, let me think. Steve came with Joe and Marty, I think they are part of the sound crew. Nick, one of the lighting crew, and Bobby from set design. There might have been others but they are the regulars so I know their names."

"Was any of them around the food?"

"No. Well, Nick came over, while I was cutting the chicken, and asked me out. But he was only there for a minute or so, he left when I said I wasn't free last evening."

"Do you know what Polyethylene Glycol is?"

"No, I've never heard of it. Is it some kind of seasoning?"

"Not exactly, it's what we found in the chicken that made everyone who ate it sick. Maybe you've heard of its other name, Miralax?"

Sandi shook her head, but would not look at the detective or the others in the tent. "Can I go now? I have to help get the breakfast cleaned up so we can start lunch."

"Okay, Sandi, that's all for now, if I have any other questions, I'll be in touch."

The group watched her leave.

Peter looked at the detective and asked, "Is that it? You aren't going to ask her if she did it."

"I don't have to; she knows more than she's saying. She made eye contact with every question except when I told her the trade name for Polyethylene Glycol. Then she became nervous and anxious to leave. Who is this Nick that she mentioned? He part of the regular crew?"

Peter shook his head. "He's one of the interns also, from Point Park. Nick Di-Marco, I don't know much about him."

"I plan on talking to all the catering crew first, then the crew who were in the tent for coffee yesterday morning. Maybe one of them saw something."

Jacob spent the rest of the morning talking to the catering staff and the five men who had been in the food tent for coffee. None of them had any idea what Polyethylene Glycol or Miralax was, or how it got into the food. Only Sandi and Tom were in charge of preparing the meat portion of lunch. Jacob was convinced Sandi knew more than she was saying. Jacob phoned Tammy and updated her on the investigation.

"Are you working on anything pressing right now?"

"No, finishing paperwork for an upcoming trial. Why, do you need me to do something?"

"Can you run a check on a Nick DiMarco? He's an intern with the film crew, attending Point Park College. No one here knows him well."

"No problem. I'll let you know what I find. Talk to you later."

Tammy hung up and began typing Nick's name into the police database. Only one hit; a driving under the influence arrest three months ago. At least she had a starting point. His driver's license was issued in Cincinnati, Ohio. She'd give the Cincinnati police a call.

After several hours of phone calls that she was certain had deformed her ear permanently, she had more information on Nick DiMarco. Since it was almost noon, she phoned Jacob and asked if he had time for lunch, and to review the new information. They agreed to meet at Legends in fifteen minutes.

Jacob arrived first and grabbed a booth in the back of the café. He ordered their drinks and lunch, as was their routine for whoever arrived for a meal first.

Tammy came in just as the waitress finished taking Jacob's order. "What did you do, run across the bridge?" Tammy asked with a laugh.

"No, just less traffic coming across the bridge than coming from Western Ave. What did you find out?"

"Nicholas DiMarco, age twenty-six from Cincinnati. Graduated high school and enlisted in the Navy. Honorable discharge in 2010. Going to Point Park for theatre arts under the GI bill. No family. Regular rebel in high school. Almost didn't graduate between suspensions and poor grades. Sounds like he had a choice either the military or jail. Seemed to have cleaned up his act though while in the Navy.

"Moved here with William Freedman, a buddy in the Navy. Freedman was a cook in the Navy, he's is going to culinary school at the Community College under the GI Bill. And interesting coincidence; Freedman is working on the catering crew for the movie."

"Isn't that just ducky?" You think Freedman might be our guy, then?"

"No, it just doesn't sound right. Freedman wasn't working yesterday. He had scheduled classes, and before you ask, I checked. He was there yesterday. Besides, he's squeaky clean, not even a parking ticket. His father is the police chief in Meadville. Although Billy didn't follow in his father's footsteps, he seems proud of him. I spoke to him this morning also, told him what was going on, and that we were going to talk to everyone from the catering staff. Chief Freedman was sure that Billy wasn't involved but, that if he was, to 'throw the book at him then send him home for me to deal with him.'" Tammy laughed as she shared that bit of information with Jacob.

"I've talked with most of the catering staff, including Freedman. He didn't strike me as our perp. He wasn't working yesterday, was in class. I checked, too. Verified by classmates and his professor. Asked him about DiMarco, said he was a good buddy, but had issues. Said Nick wanted to work on this movie for the grade and school credit, but wasn't that into it. Did say that Nick and Sandi had hooked up a few times but he didn't know how serious it was. None of the other staff triggered my gut; I don't think it was any of them. I want to keep an eye on DiMarco and Adams."

"I'll talk to Nate, between us we should be able to come up with something. You heading back to the set?"

"No, I'm heading to the office; you know if I don't write the reports as I go, they never get done. My partner used to do all that stuff, but she moved on to sex crimes so I have to do it all now," he pouted as Tammy laughed.

"I miss you, too, Jacob. Just got tired of being your secretary is all! See you later." She picked up the tab, paid the cashier, and sauntered out the door.

CHAPTER 12

"Maggie, phone."

As soon as Maggie picked up the phone, she heard the familiar buzzing that accompanied the robot voice. *"I saw him with you yesterday. I told you to stay away from him. Now you both will pay."*

The phone went dead and Maggie looked over at Amber, who had answered the phone. "Do you know who was on the phone? There was no one there when I picked up."

Amber shook her head and said that it was just some guy asking to speak to Maggie.

She finished her shift, keeping busy so she wouldn't think about the caller, but now as she was changing clothes, she let her mind drift and the voice on the phone call came back. The message made her feel edgy and her stomach was churning. She would call Tammy in the morning, there was no way to trace an incoming call to the switchboard.

She walked toward the parking garage rapidly, the wind had picked up, and it was colder than it had been that morning. She thought it might snow overnight from the look of the clouds. Maggie looked around, making sure there was no one loitering around the garage. She realized she was a little jumpy; she usually paid attention to her surroundings when she went to and from her car, but, tonight she was on high alert due to the caller. She walked up the ramp avoiding the stairs and the elevator, she shook herself believing that she was being paranoid, but she remembered the dream she had had about the garage and shivered. She frowned as she hit the remote starter. She keyed the automatic lock release and reached for the door handle, when she was grabbed from behind.

She reacted as she had been taught in her self-defense classes, stomping on the foot of her attacker and kicking his shin, although she didn't hold out hope that her duty shoes would do much damage. It did cause his grip to loosen slightly, just enough for her to turn and slam the heel of her hand into his nose, and her heel to make contact with his knee.

"You bitch," her assailant gasped as he let go of her arm.

While her assailant bent over in distress, Maggie yanked the car door open, and dove into the front seat. Once in, she locked the door put the car into gear. She pealed out of the garage, yanking out her cell phone and called Tammy. She was barely coherent and was starting to shake, her teeth were chattering, she was hiccupping, and tears were blurring her vision. Maggie pulled the car to the curb, trying to tell Tammy what had happened in the garage, she was still talking to her when a police car pulled up behind her. Tammy asked if the patrol car had arrived yet, and when Maggie said yes, Tammy said that she and Nate were on their way. One police officer came up to her window and the other went back into the garage.

"Ms. Jones? Detective Hawthorne asked me to check on your safety until she arrives. Do you need medical attention?" He seemed to be concerned that she was shaking and had difficulty speaking. "Did he hurt you?"

Maggie took a few deep breaths and was able to get her teeth to stop chattering enough to form words. "I'm not hurt; I think I hurt him, though. It's just reaction setting in; I'll be okay in a few minutes. Thank you, Officer."

As she was looking up at him, the other officer came out of the garage and shook his head. Maggie took that to mean that her attacker managed to get away.

Tammy and Nate pulled up and Tammy ran over to Maggie's car. The two police officers moved over to talk to Nate and fill him in. Maggie lurched out of the car, immediately engulfed in Tammy's arms.

"Are you all right? Can you tell me what happened?"

Maggie nodded, and pulled away, so she could keep herself under control. "I left the hospital, and walked to the garage. With everything that's been going on, I walked up the ramp, instead of using the stairs or the elevator. I had just reached for the door handle, when someone grabbed me from behind. All that self-defense stuff you and Nate made me learn worked. I never really saw his face, it was covered with a scarf when I smashed his nose, and then I only saw the top of his head when he curled over, he had a hoodie on. He's not much taller than I am; I didn't have to reach too far to hit his face. I think I broke his nose, and I heard his knee crack when I kicked it. He had black Nike running shoes, and jeans, and a black hoodie. I got in the car and drove off. Not much help, though, is it?"

Tammy looked at her in disbelief, shaking her head. "Maggie, that's more than I expected. I'll call it in and have all the hospitals check and see if anyone came through the E.D. with a broken nose or knee injury."

As Tammy called to have the local hospitals checked, Nate finished his conversation with the two patrolmen who were leaving, and came over to suggest that Maggie get checked out too; Maggie convinced him that all she really needed was to go home, take a hot shower, and get some sleep. Tammy hung up the cell phone, conveying the bad news that no one, so far, sought treatment for a broken nose or leg.

Tammy offered to drive Maggie's car home with Nate following. "Tammy, I think this was connected to the phone calls. He phoned the E.D. tonight. Said he knew that I had seen him yesterday, and that we'd both pay."

Tammy looked thoughtful for a moment, finally only nodding her head in agreement. Maggie was silent after that, she stared at the windshield but wasn't focusing on anything. They arrived at Maggie's, and Tammy saw that the lights were on, not only in the front room, but in the bath and kitchen as well. Tammy glanced over at Maggie who only stared ahead; her arms wrapped around her chest, still saying nothing. Nate pulled to the curb while Tammy drove Maggie's car to the garage.

Nate and Tammy lead the way into the house; Nate had his Glock drawn, and Tammy hung back keeping Maggie out of the way. Taser came romping toward them, tail wagging and danced around Nate, begging to be petted. Nate holstered his weapon, moving through the house with Taser on his heels.

At the foot of the stairs he started up when Tyler appeared at the landing, halting when he saw Nate. "What's happened? Maggie...."

Nate motioned for Maggie to come over to the steps so that Ty could see her for himself. He rushed down the steps examining Maggie's tear-stained and pale-as-death face. "What happened? Are you all right?"

He held her close, beseeching Tammy and Nate to fill him in on the evening's events with a look.

"There was a problem at the hospital garage tonight. Maggie was attacked, but did more damage to the attacker than he did to her. She's just shaken right now, reaction." Tyler scrutinized Tammy's face, making sure she was telling him everything.

Tammy met his gaze and nodded.

"Maggie *is* all right, she kept her head, made him hurt, and got away. She called me. He was long gone but we did find blood, Maggie broke his nose. I'm going to make tea for us. Tyler, why don't you take Maggie upstairs, get her to take a hot shower, and get comfortable?" Tammy gave him a meaningful look, and continued on into the kitchen, leaving Tyler holding Maggie, and Nate in the hall.

Tyler met Nate's eyes and cringed when Nate only shook his head and shrugged. Ty kept Maggie close to him as they went up the stairs leading her into the bath. He started the shower and helped her undress. All the while Maggie said nothing, but tears continued to stream down her face; until she at last focused on him, wrapping her arms around him, teeth chattering, and her whole body shaking.

"I was so sc…sc…scared! I heard him, and then saw his reflection in the window. I th… th…think I hurt him."

Tyler only held her close whispering comfort to her. Wishing there was something else he could do to make her feel safe. She looked up into his eyes, leaned in and kissed him. He deepened the kiss and held her close. As he ran his hands down her back, he seemed to suddenly realize that she was naked; he pulled back, gently pushing her into the shower.

"I'll be right here when you get out. Take your time, and try to relax in the shower." Ty closed the bathroom door as she stepped into the shower.

She let the hot water just pour over her until she began to feel warm again. She shampooed her hair, soaped up with her favorite vanilla shower gel, and stayed under the pelting water until it ran cold. She wrapped a towel around her hair while she rubbed herself dry and began to rub her head and hair. She went back into her bedroom to find Ty sitting on her bed. His eyes roamed over her body, and Maggie felt the heat of her blush spreading over her. Tyler simply sat there, handing Maggie sweats and a tee shirt. Maggie took them, and turned her back to him as she stepped into the sweats, pulling the shirt over her head. Tyler called her name softly, and when she turned to him, he was standing and moving toward her. When he was only a few steps away from her, he held out his arms and she moved into them, laying her head on his chest.

"I feel better now. I'm glad you were here when I got home. It helped a lot." He picked up the comb from her dresser and began to remove the tangles from her hair.

She moaned, "That feels nice."

As much as Ty would like nothing more than to stay closeted here with her, he knew Nate and Tammy were downstairs waiting for them.

Both Tammy and Nate looked up from the table when Maggie and Tyler walked in. Tammy was pouring drinks into the two glasses from the shaker sitting on the table. "I decided Cosmos with extra lime were a better choice than tea. Have a sip, then we'll discuss what happened tonight."

Maggie took her glass, and saw Nate pouring shots for him and Ty, from the bottle of Hennessey on the counter.

"I don't know what else to tell you, I told you all that I remember." Maggie looked deflated and exhausted.

"True, but let's talk about those phone calls." Nate pulled out his notebook, asking for specifics, when did they start, what was said, was it the same person, male or female?"

Maggie went to the message recorder and played the one from last night for him. It was impossible to tell if the caller was a man or woman from the distorted words emanating from the machine.

Nate asked to take the message machine with him, and Maggie readily agreed. There might be a chance to pinpoint a location, with the technology available at the crime lab.

"What about Thanksgiving? Should I cancel the dinner?" Each year, Maggie made Thanksgiving dinner for any of the nurses and residents, who didn't have family in the area and weren't able to get home for the holiday. It was more or less an open-house buffet affair; the hospital staff and police officers, who worked with Tammy and Nate, came and went as their schedule permitted. One advantage to living close to the hospital was, that even if they were on call, they could still get to Maggie's house for dinner without being too far if paged.

"Let's wait and see," Tammy replied. "Thanksgiving is still three weeks away, I would hate for it to be cancelled, everyone who has to work looks forward to it. But I don't want to make either of you a target."

"If you and Nate are both here during the day, nothing should happen. I really want to go ahead with it, maybe invite some of the out-of-town film crew as well."

Ty broke in, "You want to invite the film crew? Why?" He sounded incredulous at the thought.

"You only have Thursday off, and have to be back on set on Friday, so that doesn't leave any of you time to fly home and be back. Besides, there's more than enough food. It's a lot of people getting together and having fun. I hate the thought of someone having to eat hospital or hotel food for Thanksgiving."

"Oh," was all Tyler said. "That's a lot of work for you; you don't even know these people."

"It's no extra trouble, it's a buffet. We can talk about that later. Right now, I just want to relax, and, figure out what is going on. Do you have any ideas?"

They talked for another hour, until Maggie started to yawn. Tammy and Nate took their leave, making sure Tyler knew their phone numbers.

"I'm staying here tonight," Ty told them all. "I don't think Maggie should be alone."

No one argued with him, as he walked with them to the door. Maggie was already halfway up the stairs, calling down to say goodnight to them. She heard the dead bolt connect as Tyler closed the door, and the alarm being set.

He appeared at the bottom of the steps. "I'm going to let Taser out again and check the back door. I'll be up in a few minutes."

She finished climbing the steps, listening to Ty as he talked to Taser, while he let him out one last time.

Maggie was waiting for them as Ty and Taser entered the bedroom. She opened her arms to him, and he crawled into the big bed beside her drawing her close. He leaned in to catch her lip between his teeth, and reveled in the fact that she met his lips with hers. Their mouths broke apart, but their hands kept touching each other as they finished undressing, sinking back into the pillows.

Within moments, they were wrapped around each other. She was on fire with the need to feel him; to sink herself into him, and she acted on that desire. Her hands caressed their way down his back, and moved toward the hard length of him. He sucked in a breath as her fingers curled around him. Ty continued to kiss her neck, moving toward her breasts. Maggie's nipples peaked into hard points as his tongue laved against her, coiling deep in her core, until she felt edgy and hot, and ready to explode. Maggie arched up toward the hard ridge of Ty's erection, but he moved away, his hand entangling in the moist curls guarding the center of her being. She felt him insert a finger into her, while his thumb circled the sensitive nub in rhythm with his finger. His tongue invaded her mouth, mimicking the action of his hand. She felt everything inside her tighten to a single point of hot, pulsating need. She cried out as she exploded, wave upon wave of sensation lifting her outside of herself. Her climax caught her by surprise, and she delighted in the sensations that washed over her.

When she could breathe again, she touched his face in awe, and leaned up to kiss him. She gave him a push to move away from him, resisting his hand as he tried to hold her beside him. She moved down his body, teasing him with her mouth. She licked his nipples and lightly bit them, as she moved down, plying his torso and stomach with open-mouthed kisses, until, at last, she took the hard length of him into her mouth, using her lips to suckle him, as he had her breasts. She cupped his scrotum, as she slid her lips and tongue along the wide and pulsing vein of his hard length. She gently grated her teeth across the velvety soft tip, lapping up the drops of moisture, until she heard him growl deep in his throat and could feel him begin to lose control, his scrotum tightening and drawing up inside him. Maggie moved herself up his body straddling him.

She teased him unmercifully, rubbing herself against him, moving up and down on him, barely taking him in. He grasped her hip, and pulled her down to take him in completely. Maggie rested her hands on his chest, feeling the rapid beat of his heart. He continued to guide her, as she rode him faster and deeper, aware that he rose to meet her thrust for thrust. The tension coiled hotter, pushing her to another peak as he sat up pulling her close. Chest to chest she met him, giving as much as she took from him. Tyler growled again as Maggie drove him to the brink of insanity. The sound released something deep inside her, causing her to feel powerful and utterly feminine. She held on to his shoulders when he drove up to touch the core of her femininity.

Maggie gasped, chasing Ty up the peak, each spurring the other on, until their breath rasped and pleasure overcame them. She locked her muscles around him where they joined, feeling the spasms begin to overtake her. She contracted around him, crying out his name as waves of pleasure shot through her. The sound of his name on her lips pushed him violently over the edge. He followed her, with a groan, that ended with her name, as he pumped into her.

They sank onto their sides, still joined and kissed softly, gently. Neither of them had the strength to do more. Maggie pulled the comforter over both of them, as they lay there concentrating on breathing. Ty drew her closer, and, with her head on his chest, she made lazy circles in the light dusting of hair. He kissed the top of her head, knowing he wasn't going to be able to let her go.

"I think I died. That has never happened to me before." Maggie lifted her head. "I didn't know what I was missing."

"I take it you enjoyed that. Want to see if we can do it again?" Ty grinned at her, and nibbled on her ear.

He kissed her mouth as he moved his hand to tease her breasts, tugging the little bud until it grew pinker and harder between his fingers. He followed his hand with his mouth, teasing and biting at her nipple, all the while sliding his hand down over the soft skin of her belly to dip into her navel. She was warm and glowing with the aftermath of their loving earlier. Slowly, he followed his hand with his mouth, until he reached her hips and lifted her to him. He kissed the curve of her hip and then allowed his tongue to caress her navel. He moved lower, and she groaned with pleasure, as his mouth reached her sex. His tongue flicked across the sensitive bud that blossomed with his attention. He took her into his mouth, and feeling her buck against him, murmuring words of encouragement next to her, he urged her on until she came apart against him again. Her breath was ragged as he moved up her body, positioning himself against her. She arched up, as he entered her, in one deep thrust. The aftermath of her orgasm was still reverberating within her as he entered her, causing her to spasm against him as she climaxed yet again. The force of her orgasm clamped him to her hot velvet core. He tried to slow down, to prolong the pleasure, but she was so tight and hot, that he spurted into her, his head flung back, howling from the force of his orgasm.

He dropped against her, and she clung to him, running her hands along his back. When he moved to pull away, she rolled with him, fitting herself tight against him. They dozed and woke several times, coming together and making love, long into the night.

CHAPTER 13

They woke the next morning to clouds, and snow flurries. Ty smiled to himself, as he watched Maggie stretch and slowly open her eyes.

"Good morning."

Her expression changed as she remembered the events of the previous evening, and her skin paled then pinkened. He pulled her closer, murmured in her hair that she was fine, and he wouldn't let anything happen to her. He felt her relax in his arms and asked her what she wanted to do, since she wasn't scheduled to work.

"I'm going to do some major cleaning today, and start to get things ready for Thanksgiving. He's not going to ruin that for me. Once that's done, Tammy and I can do the shopping next week, and start preparing the food. Are you doing any of the scenes today?"

"Some, the robbery scene with the grocer. Depending on how long that takes, I may be done early. I can come by and help. My mother made sure all of us learned how to clean, cook, and do laundry. I'm pretty handy to have around the house." He gave her his lopsided grin, and Maggie couldn't help but laugh.

"I might just take you up on that. C'mon, let's get dressed, and have breakfast."

Maggie went into the bathroom, as Ty pulled on jeans and a sweatshirt. When Maggie emerged from the bath, Tyler went in. He heard Maggie talking to Taser, as she got dressed and went downstairs to the kitchen.

They worked in companionable silence, making coffee and slicing grapefruit. He filled Taser's water bowl, and laughed when he went to his food bowl, only to look reprovingly at him.

"Oh, no, you don't. You only eat once a day, and not until we both get home tonight. Silly dog," he said affectionately to the German Shepard.

Maggie watched the interaction between them and felt content. "Give him a cookie, he'll be fine."

At the word "cookie," Taser pranced to the pantry cupboard, to paw at the doorknob. Tyler opened the door, and Taser placed a big paw on the plastic container holding his treats. He opened the lid, allowing Taser to daintily pull one, large dog biscuit out of the container, and holding it gently in his mouth, went back to his corner and started to chomp on it

Maggie walked Tyler to the door shortly after, he pulled Maggie close and kissed her, hard. Maggie returned the kiss. "If you don't stop now, neither of us will get anything done today."

"I'll be home as soon as I can. Don't work too hard. Make sure the door's locked and set the alarms."

"Yes, Master." She grinned cockily at him.

"Sass? You're sassing me? I'll think of a good punishment by the time I get back. Be safe, baby." He was still laughing, as he got into his car and drove off.

CHAPTER 14

Tyler started to walk back to the roped off area, deep in thought about the scene, and getting his head back into the movie. A loud, crackling noise broke into his thoughts, he looked up to see one of the light fixtures swaying and sparking, as it tore loose from the scaffolding and began to fall directly toward him. For a moment, he was frozen to the spot, not believing what he was seeing. Finally, Tyler jumped out of the way of the massive light fixture as it shattered only a few feet away from him, exactly where he had been standing seconds before. Shards of glass and metal flew in all directions, hitting not only him, but several of the crew as well. One large piece of the crane imbedded itself in the leg of Fred, the head gaffer.

The set was in turmoil, people running toward the injured, shouting and yelling. Tyler took a deep breath as he moved toward the injured man, who was desperately trying to pull the metal shard out of his leg.

Tyler reached him and stopped him. "Fred, don't pull that out, you don't know what's injured under that. We need to get you to the hospital."

The man, Fred, looked at Ty without focusing on him. Tyler helped him to lie back, tying to keep him calm until the medics arrived. Once he was sure that an ambulance was on its way, he called Maggie and told her what had happened before it hit the news. After assuring her that he was fine, he told her that several of the crew would be heading to the hospital with various injuries.

The police arrived with the ambulance, Tyler explained what had happened, and asked if the scaffolding and light fixture could be examined; these things just didn't fall for no reason. He hated to admit it, but perhaps he was the target, the scaffolding didn't break until he was beneath it. He had no idea why he had been singled out; he couldn't think of any reason why someone would be trying to hurt him or the crew.

Since this was an external disaster, Maggie hurriedly washed up to report for duty. She was heading to the E.D., to wait for the arrival of the injured movie crew, when her cell phone rang. As soon as she picked up the phone, she knew it was the robotic caller.

"You got a good shot in last night, next time you won't get the chance. I'm still watching you, remember that."

The phone clicked and went dead. The arrival of the ambulances made Maggie put the phone call from her mind as she busily searched for Tyler, despite his assurance that he was not hurt. As soon as she saw him, she felt herself relax, forcing herself to concentrate on the injured. For the next several hours, she, and the rest of the team, worked feverishly over the crew.

Most of the crew suffered only minor injuries and were released later in the day; three of the crew's injuries were critical, however. When the light fixture fell, it took part of the crane and scaffolding with it, hurtling Paul off his perch and dropping him fifteen feet to the ground. He was the most seriously injured with head, neck, and back injuries. David had arrived, taking Paul to surgery, to remove a clot on his brain. Maggie acknowledged him while prepping Paul for surgery, but quickly moved on to see to another crewmember. Fred had been badly burned from the falling electrical wires, and had a piece of scaffolding imbedded in his leg, which severed an artery. By the time all of the movie crew had been treated, and either admitted or discharged, it was well past end of shift. She hadn't had time to think about Ty, let alone the anonymous phone call.

The police were still milling around the E.D. asking questions of the crew who had accompanied the injured men. No one had seen anything out of the ordinary. Jacob Bowen had been there most of the day, and came over to Maggie with a cup of bitter hospital coffee. "Seems as if your caller has upped his game. He's not happy just tampering with laxatives, now. Someone could have been killed today, and almost was."

"I know. I wish I knew who he was. Do you think he's the same person behind Ty's abduction? It seems as if someone doesn't want this movie to be made."

Bowen looked as if he had been struck with lightning. "What makes you say that?"

"For one, he was abducted and injured. Not too many people knew he was in Pittsburgh yet. Then, the food tampering occurred to make everyone sick. Now, the crane's failure. And, in between, the calls to me warning me to stay away from him. It sounds as if he's against anyone connected to the movie not just Tyler."

"You may have a point, Maggie. I'll run another check on the crew, especially our interns. How are you doing? I heard about what happened last night. You did good, fighting him off."

"Jacob, I got another call on my way to the hospital today, on my cell phone. That's not a number many people have. The same nonsense as before, but I think it was him last night, he told me I got a good shot at him, but next time I won't get the chance."

"He's getting angry. Nothing has gone exactly as he hoped, Ty's fine, and the movie is still on schedule. I'll be in touch." Jacob left, nodding to a few of the remaining police officers.

Maggie looked around to see that everything was in order, then traversed the length of the treatment area to the locker room. On the bench just outside the door, she found Tyler waiting for her.

"So much for cleaning your house." He smirked at her.

"There's always next week. Or, with the overtime, I can hire someone to come in and clean everything, including the walls and floors. Mmmmmmm, not a bad idea, then I can have more time to cook and bake for the holidays." She grinned at him, taking his hand to lead him out of the hospital. "Where's your car?"

"At the shoot."

"No problem, I'll drive you home, and you can pick up your car in the morning."

"Which home are you driving me to, yours or mine?"

"Where do you want to go?"

"With you, of course."

They reached her truck and climbed in, unaware that they were being watched from a room in the hospital.

CHAPTER 15

Things quieted down for the next few days. Maggie breathed a sigh of relief, no phone calls, and no more "accidents" on the set. Despite what she had threatened, she cleaned the house herself, including the carpets, floors, and walls. Ty was busy with the movie, opting to go to the hotel afterward, due to the late, or rather, early morning hours of the escape footage. They saw little of each other, but texted or talked several times a day during breaks.

Maggie was secretly glad for the break, she was still unsure of how this would end. She knew his life was in L.A. She really did not anticipate moving there; not that he'd asked her. Her life and roots were here, she couldn't see how she could cope with the paparazzi, the tabloids, and the whole L.A. scene. The ringing of the telephone broke her out of her reverie. She was a little apprehensive as she answered it, but as she glanced at the caller I.D. she smiled.

"Hey, Tammy, what's up?"

"Are you still planning to host Thanksgiving?"

"Sure, why?"

"I'm heading to HGS warehouse, want to come and save a little money?"

"I'm not dressed, I've been cleaning. How soon are you leaving?"

"Go get dressed, I'm finishing my coffee. Twenty minutes enough time?"

"Absolutely! See you then."

Maggie tore up the stairs to her bath, shedding clothes as she went. Fifteen minutes later, she was showered and dressed. While waiting for Tammy, she texted Tyler: "Gone shopping with Tammy, talk to you later."

She and Tammy caught up while strolling through the aisles of HGS. Tammy was getting necessary items for baking and making Christmas dinner.

"You are going to have dinner with us on Christmas Day, aren't you?"

"Probably not, I signed up for an extra shift on Christmas."

"Maggie, why do you do that? We ask you every year to have dinner with us. Why do you insist on working a double on the holidays?"

"Tammy, you know why. I don't have any family, and it makes it a little easier for those who do. If it makes you any happier, I have Christmas Eve off. The rest of the staff drew straws to see who would work, no one would let me sign up for a shift then, since I'm working two on Christmas Day. So, how about we share dinner then?"

Tammy sighed, but smiled at her and nodded. "Okay, I'll hold you to that. What else do you need in this aisle?"

Maggie picked up a large package of brown sugar, walnuts, flour, graham cracker crumbs, coconut, chocolate chips, and vanilla extract. She looked at the other items in the cart: two forty-pound turkeys, two whole hams, a large roast, ricotta cheese, lasagna noodles, ground meat, and the other ingredients for marinara sauce; she had potatoes, sharp cheddar cheese, fresh vegetables and various fresh herbs. "I think I got everything I need for Thanksgiving dinner. Just let me pick up some sterno for the warming trays, paper plates, utensils, and napkins."

They wandered through the large warehouse, looking for possible gifts for the Toys for Tots® Drive. They picked up a variety of items, then headed to the cashier. As they exited the warehouse store, they discussed where to go for lunch.

Maggie was lowering the tailgate, when she heard the whining of an engine racing. She and Tammy looked up at the same time to see an SUV careening out of control and heading straight toward them. Tammy jumped to the front of the pickup, Maggie leapt into the truck bed. The SUV slammed into the tailgate and spun completely around, allowing the rear of the SUV to hit the tailgate again. Maggie felt the truck quake from the force of the impact. The tailgate shrieked as if in pain, as it twisted around the SUV's bumper.

The driver's side door opened, and a figure, in a black hoodie and jeans burst out, began running, in a lopsided way, toward the center of the parking lot. People shouted at him to stop, and one stalwart man began to chase after him.

Tammy ran to the back of the pickup, shouting Maggie's name. She spied Maggie leaning against the rear cab window. She caught Tammy's eye and said, "How am I going to explain THIS to the rental and insurance companies?" She started to giggle, but clamped down to stop herself. She was afraid if she started, she would never quit. She slowly crawled toward the twisted tailgate and hopped down.

Tammy was on her cell, talking to Jacob. The wail of sirens filled the air, as police and fire vehicles pulled into the lot.

The man who had given chase, Thomas Marcus, trotted back out of breath. "I couldn't catch up to him, but I did see the car he got into. A green Olds, with a PA license plate HML4200. I should have been able to catch him, considering the limp he had. Must be getting old," he muttered, and Tammy thanked him for his effort, saying that the license would be a big help.

Jacob wrote down his contact information, and gave Mr. Marcus his card. One of the patrol officers read out the license and vehicle description for an all points alert. Two of the firefighters pushed the tailgate semi-closed and tied it to the frame.

Maggie gave the keys to Tammy. "I don't think I can drive right now; can you drive us home?" she asked, her voice wavering.

Jacob took the keys from Tammy. "I don't think either of you are in any condition to drive. McHenry can follow us in my car."

As they drove home, Jacob filled them in on what he had found out, which wasn't much. "Cincinnati police confirmed what we already knew. Since the Navy and starting college, DiMarco hasn't had so much as a parking ticket. He hasn't missed a day of work, or class. He was seeing Sandi Adams occasionally, didn't seem to be serious though. Doesn't socialize much with the rest of the crew, went out for a few drinks on payday with them, but nothing more."

"So this is another dead end?" Maggie asked.

"Not necessarily. You know how after a crime the neighbors all say, 'He was such a polite, quiet young man,' this could be the same thing. Something triggered this. Tyler, the movie, I'm not sure but something," Jacob replied. "We're still looking into it. Here we are, I'll talk to you both later."

When they reached Maggie's street, reporters surrounded the house. Maggie blanched, looking wildly at Tammy and Jacob.

"What's going on? Why are they all here?" Maggie's voice was tremulous as she took in the crowd on the sidewalk in front of her home.

"Best guess is that they heard about the incident at the parking lot," Tammy answered.

"But that's not newsworthy! Unless it's because a police officer was involved."

Tammy gave her a look that said that the media blitz had everything to do with her and Tyler and not an off-duty police officer.

They didn't have long to wonder, because, as soon as they stepped out of the truck, a cacophony of voiced questions barraged them. All clamoring for Maggie, was it true that she was dating Ty Sinclair, and that she was targeted as well as the movie set? Did she have any enemies, who would want to run her down? The questions came nonstop, the reporters began to crowd around her as she moved toward her porch. Tammy and Jacob ran interference, and kept up a monologue of "No comment" as they pushed through the crowd. Finally, when they reached the front door, Jacob took the keys from Maggie's shaking hand, opened it, and pushed her inside.

Maggie sank down onto the sofa. "What was that? How did they find me?"

"Not too hard, they have contacts at the station; it would be easy to find out who you were." Jacob answered her, inwardly cursing that he hadn't foreseen this and prevented Maggie from being accosted by the media.

"But how did they know about Tyler? The station wouldn't know that we're seeing each other, that's not in any of the reports you and Jake made."

"Good point," Tammy said as she switched on the TV and turned to the news.

The weather report was just finishing and the anchor smiled into the camera.

"Now for breaking news, as we reported at the beginning of the newscast, there was an attempt on the life of Tyler Sinclair's new girlfriend. An anonymous source told us that Maggie Jones, an emergency room nurse, and part of the Pittsburgh Film Office Medical Team, was almost killed when an SUV drove straight at her in the Pittsburgh Mills Mall complex earlier this morning. Ms. Jones was able to dive out of the way of the oncoming vehicle, and is reportedly uninjured. It is not known how or when Tyler and Ms. Jones met, our source did indicate that they met when Ty was injured a few weeks ago, during the freak snowstorm that hit the area. When we have more information, we will bring it to you. Now to Jordy Rand, with sports."

Maggie turned off the TV in disgust. "It has to be the caller. Only you two and Nate know I'm seeing Tyler. And, Mike, of course but he wouldn't say anything, it might hurt Ty's image. Do you think the caller was behind the almost accident?"

Jacob looked askance at her. "Did you just think of that now? That was my first thought when we found out that the SUV had been reported stolen last night."

"Was he trying to kill me or just scare me again?

"My guess, just scare you. He veered off slightly just before impact."

The phone began ringing and Tammy grabbed it after seeing the color drain from Maggie's face. "Hello, Jones residence."

"Tammy? Is Maggie all right? It's Ty."

"Yes, she's right here, I'm screening calls. The press is outside. Hold on, here she is."

"Maggie, I just heard on TV. Are you okay?"

"Physically, yeah. Emotionally, I'm a mess. My house has turned into a media frenzy. I'm so sorry, they asked about our relationship. We didn't answer the question. I never said anything to anyone but Nate, Tammy, and Jake. I'm so...."

"Maggie, honey, stop. I know you wouldn't invite this chaos into your life. What do Jake and Tammy say?"

"They think it's the caller. That somehow, he knows about us, and was the anonymous tipster to the TV station. KDKA broke the news first. They're trying to find out how the tip was made. However, I'm not holding out any hope that they find anyone. Will this make any trouble for you?"

"No, I'm used to dodging the press. I'll tell them whatever makes it easier for you. Do you want me to tell them that we are together? It would mean that you may be hounded by the press; I would ask them not to harass you, but they don't always cooperate. On the other hand, if I say, 'No comment,' they'll draw their own conclusions. The last choice is that I deny that we are seeing each other."

"What happens if we admit we're seeing each other and give them the details of how we met? Would they leave us alone?"

"It's a possibility. I could tell one of them that I'll give them an exclusive, if, after the story, they agree to my terms which will be to leave you alone."

"What about you? Won't they hound you?"

"I can handle that. And so can Mike."

"Mike'll be furious if you do that. Ty, what do you want to do?"

He laughed. "Well, if I tell them we're together, then, maybe you'll start to believe it."

Maggie sputtered into the phone. He continued to laugh, Maggie began to laugh with him.

"Well, honey, what do I tell the press? Are we together?" Ty held his breath, waiting for her answer.

"Yes, we're together. I'll let you handle it."

They said goodbye and hung up.

Maggie turned to the others and grinned at them. "I suppose you heard all that. I guess it's a good idea, he IS used to dealing with them. Maybe they'll let me alone now."

Once the media frenzy died down, Tammy and Maggie unloaded the truck, and began putting things away.

Tyler was smiling to himself, as he called Mike, to have him set up a press conference. As expected, Mike wasn't happy when Ty told him it was about Maggie. Mike gave him several reasons for not announcing they were a couple. After listening to Mike's arguments, Tyler had heard enough and threatened to find a new agent if Mike continued to be hostile to Maggie.

"You don't even know her and have made no attempt to get to know her. This is MY decision and I will talk to the press, with or without you."

Mike knew he had to stop his opposition to Maggie. "Look, Ty, you're right, I don't know her. I do trust your judgment, though, so go ahead, talk to the media about her. If it will make you happy, I'll take you both to dinner tonight, so I can get to know her."

Ty only shook his head at his friend. "We'll talk about that later. For now just arrange this for me."

CHAPTER 16

The press conference where Ty confirmed that, yes, he had been in a car accident due to the snowstorm, but thanks to a nurse named Maggie, he was fine, started at four-fifteen. Yes, he and Maggie were seeing each other socially. Maggie wasn't used to dealing with the press and since the relationship was in its beginning stages, Tyler asked if they would give Maggie a chance to get used to him before the press scared her off. Most of them laughed, some even wished him well. A few asked if he and Maggie would pose for pictures. Tyler said he wouldn't make any promises, but would talk to her about that. It was over in thirty minutes, Ty made his way back to his room. He wanted to call Maggie and see if she was up for dinner with Mike this evening.

Then one smarmy reporter, following them into the hotel lobby called out, "How do the anonymous phone calls fit in?"

Ty turned his head to see who had asked the question, but continued to walk toward the bank of elevators ignoring the man.

The reporter continued to follow him. "Do the phone calls have anything to do with your abduction?"

"Abduction?" Ty finally turned to the reporter, Mike beside him.

"I received a tip that you'd been abducted the day you got into town. Just like I did this morning about your girlfriend. Both tips mentioned the calls she's been getting. So what's the deal? Were you carjacked when you first got here? Any ideas who would want to do that, was there a ransom demand? How does your new girlfriend fit in to all this?"

The way he kept saying "girlfriend" made Ty uneasy, there was something weird about this reporter.

"Look, I don't know where you got your information, but I wasn't abducted. If you have anything else you want to know or comment on, contact the police." Tyler turned his back on the reporter and got into the elevator.

Mike kept the reporter from following.

Mike watched the reporter leave the hotel, getting on the next elevator to Ty's floor. "You're usually better with the press than today. What is going on?" Mike eyed Ty with concern.

"There was something about him. The tone of voice when he said 'girlfriend,' as if he knew more than he was saying. He never said where he was from either."

"He must be from KDKA; they're the ones who broke the story about Maggie's near miss this morning, based on an anonymous tip. Want me to find out his name?"

"Might not be a bad idea. Do it tomorrow, tonight, let's just go to dinner and have a good time. I want you to get to know Maggie."

Mike grunted, but left Ty alone to shower and dress, retreating to his room across the hall. A quarter of an hour later, Ty reentered the sitting room and called Maggie. He smiled at the idea of taking Maggie out to dinner and spending time with Mike.

Maggie took her time getting ready for dinner. She usually didn't wear much makeup, but, tonight she took pains with her eyes. The dress she chose was a deep burgundy and clung to her figure like a caress, but was otherwise conservative. She didn't' usually wear heels, tonight, though, she wanted the added confidence that the two-inch heels would yield. She hoped that once Michael knew her better, he wouldn't be as hostile.

Shortly after eight, a limo pulled up in front of her house. She watched as Ty got out of the car, loping up the steps to her, clutching her to him and kissing her senseless when he got to the door.

She pulled away, grinned at him. "I needed that to distract me from what is coming."

"It's not going to be as bad as all that." Ty took her coat from the hook and helped her on with it. "Shall we get this over with? The sooner we do, the sooner we can be alone." He wiggled his eyebrows in a leering manner, and twirled an imaginary mustache.

Maggie giggled as they exited the house, walking toward the car. Mike genuinely smiled at her as she entered the rear seat, remarking on how lovely her dress was. He had made reservations for the three of them at Bravo Trattoria, a small, intimate Italian restaurant in the Strip District.

They followed the maître d' to a cozy table near the rear of the restaurant, where a plate of antipasto waited in the center, allowing the waiter to take their drink order. Maggie had been here only once, for a Christmas party hosted by one of the transplant surgeons for his team, but, that had been in the private dining room upstairs. This was so much nicer, Maggie thought. The room was dimly lit, but there was enough light at the tables to easily read the menu. Red-and–white-checked tablecloths covered the tables, the walls were a pale, sunset rose color. Soft strains of music floated through the room, enough to distinguish the melody, but not loud enough to interfere with conversation. Maggie began to relax against the banquette, sipping the slightly sweet white wine. She felt Michael's eyes on her, and lifted hers to meet him head-on. Michael had the good grace to look away, Maggie felt the heat of a blush on her cheeks. Tyler was not unaware of the byplay between them, and cleared his throat.

"Michael, I believe there were some things you wanted to say to Maggie?"

It was Michael's turn to flush as he turned to Maggie. "I wanted to apologize for the comments I made when Ty was in the Emergency Department. I realize how they could have been misinterpreted."

Maggie's mouth dropped open, she just stared at Michael for a few seconds. "Misinterpreted? I don't think I misinterpreted your comments on how I would gain a great deal of money for peddling my story of Ty's accident to the tabloids. Nor did I misinterpret how you looked down your nose at me when he told you he was interested in me. As far as I am concerned, your apology leaves much to be desired." Although Maggie's voice was low, there was no mistaking the anger she held in tight control. "If that is why you arranged this dinner, to ease your con-science, then I believe the evening is over."

She turned to Ty and glared at him, trying to get him to move, so she could get out of the booth. He merely sat there staring into Maggie's face.

Finally, he took her hands in his and leaned close to her, so that only she would hear him. "Baby, don't leave. He's not very good at apologies; in fact, he never makes them." She could feel his lips turn up in a smile against her neck. "When he does apologize, no matter how muddled it is, he truly means it."

Tyler's lips were soft against her neck as he kissed her, just behind her ear, and she shivered from the sensation. He pulled back to look at her again, then turned to Michael. "She is right, you know, there was no misinterpreting your com-ments. I wanted you both to get to know each other so you could each see that the other isn't the enemy."

Michael had the grace to look embarrassed. Maggie wondered if she should offer her own apology, when Michael spoke.

"Maggie, Ty's right. That wasn't a very sincere apology. I did misjudge you at the hospital. I was worried about him and after you gave me a dressing down, I find out that you were the one who rescued him. I'm used to dealing with people who have an angle, and thought you were no different. After hearing what's been going on, I find myself admitting that I'm wrong. Please forgive me. I'd like to start over if you're amenable." He held his hand out to her and she took it, giving him a wide smile.

"I'd like nothing more than to start over. I'm a little sensitive about people jumping to conclusions. Perhaps I overreacted, as well. You are aware that I've invited the cast and crew who are staying in Pittsburgh for Thanksgiving dinner. If you are going to be here, I'd like to invite you to join us." Michael gave her a real smile this time and told her he'd be delighted.

Dinner continued amid much discussion about football—who was better the Steelers or the Rams? Books—they all agreed that the *Millennium* trilogy was the best; movies—why did they remake old classics and ruin them or worse yet, colorize them? The evening flew by and Maggie stifled a yawn but not before Ty caught part of it. He looked at his watch and signaled for the check.

Michael looked askance at him, waiting for an explanation. "Maggie is working the early shift tomorrow, it's almost eleven o'clock, and she needs to get home and sleep."

Maggie was startled when she heard what time it was. She slid out of the booth behind Ty and thanked Michael for a nice evening. Michael asked if they could do it again.

Maggie nodded, smiling. "I'd like that, Michael. Thank you."

She offered her hand to him but to her added surprise, he rose and kissed her on the cheek. The three of them left the restaurant in a companionable silence that wasn't broken, until the limo pulled up in front of Maggie's house. Michael got out and helped Maggie exit the car; he leaned down and kissed her cheek.

"Goodnight, Maggie. Be safe."

He climbed back into the limo, Tyler held her hand as they walked up to the front door. The limo's quietly purring engine faded into the distance as it drove back to the hotel with Michael. Ty took the key from her hand and together they entered her house, neither noticing the van parked across the street with malevolent eyes watching.

CHAPTER 17

The next few weeks passed in a flurry of activity. The movie was progressing with no farther incidents. The crew all breathed a collective sigh of relief. Maggie was busy as well. As soon as she returned home from work, she was busy cooking and baking for the Thanksgiving open house. There were no farther phone calls, either. Maggie wasn't sure she was relieved or not; the caller could just be taking a break, priming himself to start the calls again.

Tyler spent most nights with Maggie, she was beginning to get used to him being there. She wanted to be happy with the way things were going, but she also knew that once the movie was finished, he would be returning to L.A., and she would remain here. She resolved not to dwell on that, just to take pleasure in the here and now.

Thanksgiving dawned cold and sunny. With the Macy's Parade on the TV as background noise, Maggie made last minute preparations for the first wave of luncheon guests. The serving areas were set up, and soon would be filled with the turkey, beef, and ham slices. The other compartments would hold the lasagna and vegetables. Baskets of rolls were placed strategically around the room. Coolers were set up holding water, sodas, and beers for those who were off duty. The desserts were in the kitchen for later as was the coffee urn.

The first guests arrived at twelve-thirty, and, after greeting Maggie, some with gifts like wine, candy, or flowers, made a beeline for the food. Most of them sat around the dining room table, or on chairs with tables in the sitting room. There was a never-ending line of people coming and going. The house was full of laughter and conversation; all the various groups seemed to be getting along well.

Tyler arrived about three o'clock with Michael and Sal. Ty pulled her into a warm embrace, kissing her intensely. Both men greeted her warmly, Michael even bringing a bottle of wine for her, his previous animosity seemed to have vanished. Jacob and Tammy got there shortly afterward, and they discussed how there had been no farther events to shut down production during the past two weeks. As they continued to discuss the movie, and how it was winding down, loud voices erupted from the dining room, accompanied by the sound of crashing furniture and breaking glass. Maggie groaned, she and Tammy running toward the dining room. Broken dishes, remnants of food, and glass littered the floor, scattered among overturned chairs. One of the movie crew was nose-to-nose and yelling at one of the doctors. Maggie stepped forward to the two men, but Jacob pulled her back and advanced on the combatants.

"All right, gentlemen, break it up. You're not in a bar but in someone's home. I'm sure you don't want to spend the night in jail for disorderly conduct, and whatever else I can think of, if Ms. Jones wants to press charges for destruction of private property. I need your names and then you can tell me what this is all about?"

The doctor spoke up. "I'm Rob Simmons and I don't know what happened; we were talking about the movie and how closely it reflects the actual events. He blew up, said we all had the story wrong. He took a swing at a couple of the others and knocked over the chairs, and the old guy over there dropped his plate and glass."

Jacob turned to the presumed instigator of the heated discussion for his version of the story.

"Nick DiMarco, well, well. I suppose I shouldn't be too surprised to see you in the middle of this. Now, why don't you tell me why you're destroying Ms. Jones' home, when she so graciously invited you for Thanksgiving dinner."

Jake was deliberately baiting Nick to see how he would react. Surprisingly, Nick remained calm.

"Look, these dumb shits think that Kate Soffel was misunderstood and a victim. She caused the whole problem. She destroyed her family because she was a vain and selfish bitch. She deserved what she got, and it certainly isn't a movie making her the injured party. Her husband was the victim, yet this movie is making is seem as if he were behind the whole escape plot to get rid of her."

"What makes you such an authority on Kate Soffel?"

"I've heard all the stories, the popular ones, and the ones no one knows. I'm just tired of people making her the victim. What about her children? What they had to suffer?" Nick's voice was getting louder as he ranted, and Jake wanted to keep the scene from escalating again.

"Nick, no one doubts that she wasn't very circumspect when it came to the Biddle brothers. This isn't the place to discuss it, the actors and the crew of the movie have nothing to do with why the movie is being made, or even how it's being interpreted. They're only doing the jobs they were hired to do. Now, you have two choices: apologize to Maggie and help clean up this mess so we can all get back to the party, or I'm hauling you in for drunk and disorderly. It's up to you, Maggie said she isn't going to press charges, but I still can. We will talk more about this tomorrow at the station, say around eleven?"

Nick had the grace to flush, as he looked over at Maggie, who was standing in the doorway of the dining room. Her face was pale he thought she looked sad as she surveyed the broken plates and food strewn about the floor. He bent over and began to pick up the ruined food, paper plates, and utensils.

"Maggie, I'm sorry. I lost my temper. I'll get this all cleaned up; just show me where you keep the vacuum and cleaning supplies."

Maggie nodded and left the room to get the supplies. She fully intended to let him clean up the mess by himself. Tammy came up behind her, taking the bucket and cleaning things to the dining room along with a broom, and handed them to Nick.

"Can't very well use the vacuum on the wood floors," she told him softly, "they'll scratch the finish, and these are original floors. Maggie's great-great-grandfather built this house before the Kate Soffel incident. He sanded the floors by hand, there were no electric sanders then."

Nick looked up at her, then looked all around the room in amazement. "Really? Her family has lived here all that time?"

Tammy nodded. Nick mumbled something under his breath, Tammy couldn't make it out, and began to sweep the smaller pieces of debris together. He worked diligently and within a quarter hour, that area of the dining room gleamed. Maggie came over to him then and thanked him for cleaning the mess.

"I made it, you were only right in making me clean it." She smiled at him and handed him a plate. "Go, eat, but make sure it goes into your stomach stomach this time and not the floor"

Nick laughed, as he headed toward the buffet table.

"That was generous of you," Nate said behind her. "I would have thrown his ass out."

"Initially I wanted to, but he did apologize, and did a great job of cleaning it all up. I may hire him to clean all the floors," she joked as two solid arms came around her and hugged her close. She turned in the securing arms and smiled up at Ty. "Hi."

"Hi yourself, is this how your soirées usually end up, as a brawl? I thought you were 'such a nice, quiet individual.'"

"I thought I'd do something different this year. Needed to spice things up a bit, it's been way too dull the past few weeks. No stalker phone calls, nothing going wrong on the movie set, we needed some excitement." She giggled as she hugged him back.

Tyler leaned in to kiss her deeply, only to be interrupted by someone clearing their throat behind them. "Don't you two think you're a little old for such blatant PDAs?"

Maggie blushed but didn't let go of Ty. Tammy grinned at them as she and Nate went back to the buffet and began to fill their plates. Maggie and Ty went around the room making sure everyone had enough to eat, introducing the movie crew to the hospital staff, and generally acting as hosts. Maggie faltered as she saw David talking to one of the residents on his service, she didn't go talk to him, although she wondered why he was here and not at home with Linda. She let that thought go as she and Tyler ate their meal. She couldn't get the smile off her face as they talked to everyone and refilled the buffet table. She thought that this was the best Thanksgiving dinner she'd ever hosted.

Eventually everyone left, most of the guests clearing away their own dishes. Maggie had dinner plate containers of leftovers prepared by the door, and told everyone to help themselves as they left. "I can't possibly eat all of this, and it will go to waste. You will have enough for lunch or dinner tomorrow."

The hospital staff hugged her as they left and the movie crew took their cue from them, hugging Maggie and shaking hands with Ty. There were many comments of "Thank you," and "Great dinner" as the door closed behind the last guest. Since she had made plates for everyone, there wasn't much left to clear away. What the guests didn't take, Nate bagged up and took to the police station for the night crew to munch on. Most of them had come to Maggie's dinner in other years; they all looked forward to the treat.

Once everything was bagged, and cleared away, and Nate and Tammy said goodnight, Ty pulled Maggie into the living room. They curled up together on the sofa, turning the stereo on quietly. They just sat there cuddling, enjoying the quiet after the hectic afternoon and evening. The quiet was disrupted by the sound of breaking glass, followed by the klaxon of the alarm. Maggie screamed and jumped up from the sofa. Taser charged down the steps toward the front door, the three of them reached the door together. The brick lying on the floor shattered the center leaded-glass panel. Maggie bent to pick it up.

Ty stopped her. "Leave it; the note wrapped around it may have his fingerprints on it." He pulled his phone out of his jean pocket and called the police. After explaining what had happened he hung up.

Seconds later, Maggie's phone began ringing, she sighed as she saw the caller I.D. "It's Tammy," she told Ty, as she picked up the phone. "Hi, we're fine. There's a note on the brick that I haven't read yet; Ty wanted the police to see if there are any fingerprints on the paper. You know as well as I do that there won't be any."

Tammy said that she and Nate would be down in a few minutes. They arrived before the police, but when the cruisers did come, there were two cars and a crime-scene crew. Nate must have called in some favors to get this kind of response for a broken window; or maybe, it wasn't Nate at all, but the fact that Tyler was the one who called, the city didn't want negative publicity where Hollywood was concerned.

When did I become so cynical? Maggie berated herself.

They gave their statements to the officer, and the forensic team bagged the brick and letter separately. They gave the plastic bag to Maggie to read, she wished they hadn't

I warned you: Stay away from him. What do I have to do to keep you away from him?

"Maggie, I think it's time you thought about going somewhere for a while. You're too exposed here." Tammy spoke in a low voice so the men wouldn't hear. "I also think you might want to distance yourself from Ty until we find who's behind these threats."

"Tammy, I can't leave here; it's my home. Besides, there's Taser, where could I go that I can take him? Don't say you and Nate can babysit, your schedules are worse than mine. Why would I want to stay away from him?" she asked, pointing to Ty.

"Just give it a thought. I hate to think of you here alone." Maggie saw the genuine concern on her friend's face.

"I have Taser, and the alarm is set; it was set when all this started. Look how fast you all responded."

Neither heard the men come into the hallway.

"Besides, I'll be here with her," Tyler said, putting his arm around Maggie's shoulders.

"Ty, I don't think that's a good idea. When you're around that's when Maggie is most vulnerable. My professional opinion is that you need to stay away from each other, at least until we get this creep."

"You really think it's the two of us together that sets him off?" Ty looked from Nate to Tammy. "What are you thinking?"

"I'm not sure. I'm just saying that things escalate, when the two of you are together. Whoever our guy is, he's not too happy with you. I just think that having you separate may draw him out."

Tyler looked over to Nate, trying to reason with him instead of Tammy, who was acting like a mother lioness with her cubs where Maggie was concerned. "Nate, that doesn't make too much sense, if our being together upsets him, then it's better for us to stay together; that's how we'll draw him out."

Nate studied Ty for a few minutes and then turned slowly to face Tammy. "He's probably right, Tam, let's face it. If it *is* the two of them that makes our guy act out, we'll just have to control the situation." Nate turned to Tyler and Maggie. "You two will have to do everything we tell you. That means changing routes to and from work, shopping, anywhere you go. I don't want you sticking to a routine. Maggie, leave for work at a slightly different time, leave early and take a roundabout route; go to lunch at a different time than you normally do, or at least make sure you stay with hospital staff. One thing we are sure of is that he isn't part of the hospital. He hasn't hit here yet, just on the movie set, which makes me believe he's part of one of the crews. For now, Ty, you take care of her, or you'll have to answer to us." He tried to look fierce, but the corners of his mouth wouldn't cooperate.

With the debris cleaned, and the door boarded up, Nate and Tammy left. Maggie reset the alarm, and Taser followed Ty around the house, making sure nothing else was out of place. Arm in arm, they dragged up the stairs to bed and tried to sleep. Maggie lay still and tried to slow her breathing, not wanting Ty to know she wasn't asleep, thinking about what Tammy had said. She didn't want anything else to happen to Tyler, and she was afraid that if they stayed together, something would. She punched the pillow and closed her eyes, trying to breathe slowly.

"Maggie, turn your brain off, I can hear it over here." He rolled toward her and hooked an arm around her waist. "Tell me what you're thinking."

Maggie rolled over to face him. "Tyler, I'm afraid. He's getting more out of control. What's to say that next time, he won't do something worse? What if Tammy's right, maybe we should stay away from each other for a while. "

He felt his chest tighten as she spoke. This couldn't be happening, he knew he was in love with Maggie, and couldn't bear the thought of not being with her every day. He understood Tammy's view, and he knew that if anything happened to Maggie, he wouldn't be able to live with himself. But, to give her up, he didn't think he was strong enough to do that. Besides, what could they do that would be convincing, he had just told the paparazzi that he was in love with her. He was being selfish, not wanting to give her up; Tammy was right, he needed to keep her safe. The set had security all the time, and he had a driver if he wanted one, to and from the hotel, but she was just out there where any nut job could get to her. He finally realized that what Tammy was proposing was right. Nate and Tammy would be able to keep an eye on her. He pulled her close, kissing her deeply, all the while putting his plan into motion. He knew that he had to do whatever he could to keep her safe.

CHAPTER 18

Tammy was awakened to the chirp of her cell phone, and examined the caller I.D. "Hello, Ty. Everything all right?"

Tyler took a deep breath, this was tearing his heart out, and he knew what effect it would have on Maggie. "Tammy, you're right. I need to keep my distance from Maggie. She already knows I'm flying home for a few days, since I'm not on the shooting schedule, for the premiere of *Dragonfire*. While I'm there, I'll be seeing some old friends as well, by friends I mean females, that I've been seen with in the past. They really are just friends, and we've helped each other previously for red carpet appearances, and premiers, and such. One of them, my costar in *Dragonfire*, will be with me for the premier, and we've been linked to each other in the past. I've already talked to her about renewing our 'friendship,' and she's agreed. I know this is going to crush Maggie, but she needs to think I'm really a bastard, and that this was a setup to get Heidi back. Can you and Nate keep her safe?" He heard his voice crack on the last word.

"Tyler, as much as I think you and Maggie need to keep your distance until we catch this nut job, I'm not sure hurting her like this is the best way. You know she has trust issues, and I'm not sure she'll be able to forgive you, if you proceed with this crazy plan. Maybe just being away for will have the same results."

"I'll have to risk that. If the caller thinks we broke up, maybe he'll let her alone. She means too much to put her in jeopardy because of the film and me. When this is over, I'll explain everything. If she won't listen, then at least I'll know she's safe."

Tammy, then Nate tried to talk Ty out of his plan, but he was adamant; finally, they both agreed to help Maggie through his "unfaithfulness" while in L.A. He hung up, feeling as if part of his heart had been ripped away. He made his way back up to the bedroom, where Maggie was still curled up under the comforter, and crawled back into bed with her. He pulled her close and she sighed against his chest. He stayed awake watching her sleep, memorizing each precious feature and sound that she made. When the alarm rang for Maggie to get ready for work, he was still watching her as she stretched and blinked awake.

When she met his eyes, she smiled and reached up to kiss him. "Why didn't you wake me?" she purred as she snuggled closer to his chest.

"You looked so adorable sleeping, that I lost track of time just watching you." He kissed her hair and held her closer. "You know I'm flying out to L.A. this morning, right? I don't want to leave you, but I do have to take care of some things personally, like the premiere of *Dragonfire*. The next few weeks will be hectic, I have to do publicity for that movie, and fit the shooting schedule in as well. "

"I know, but you'll call me every night, so that'll be okay. The sooner you go and take care of what you need to do for *Dragonfire*, the sooner you'll be back. Besides, I'll be working late the rest of the week, getting ready for the hospital's accreditation visit. All I'll be doing is working, eating, sleeping, and counting the hours until you get back." She grinned at him and reluctantly pulled away to get ready for work. "Want to shower with me?" she asked coyly as she sashayed into the bathroom.

Tyler debated for only a second and decided he needed to be with her one last time before he hurt her, possibly irrevocably. He followed her into the shower, poured shampoo into his hands and began to massage the shampoo into her hair. She moaned softly as his fingers massaged her scalp, pulling gently through the silky stands. She wrapped her arms around his neck and kissed him passionately, as the water cascaded over her hair, rinsing the shampoo from it.

Ty reached past her and grabbed the bottle of shower gel; he poured some over Maggie's back and began swirling it in circles over her skin. He pulled away from her and began to slowly wash her all over. As he brushed against her breast, she felt her nipples harden from the contact, and her stomach clenched as he moved lower down her abdomen. She moved her hands over his firm chest and abdomen, making her way to his already hard arousal. Her fingers teased his length and sac, making him suck his breath in harshly. He moved her farther into the streaming water to rinse her completely, as he continued to push her against the tile of the shower, lifting her slightly, until his engorged penis was lined up with her core.

He lowered Maggie slowly, until he nudged her entrance and felt her heat. Ty leaned toward her and kissed her, as he surged into her. She whimpered against his lips and the vibration caused him to moan in response, as he began to move her up and down on him. He knew she was close, because the whimpers became louder and she was twisting trying to get closer to him. Tyler was relentless, moving faster and harder against her, until he felt her contact against him; she pulled her mouth away from him and sobbed from the pleasure. The contraction of her muscles brought him over, and he tipped his head back to roar his release.

He lowered her until her feet were firmly under her and held her close. "I love you, Maggie. Always know that. I'll always love you."

Maggie gazed into his troubled eyes and frowned. "Tyler, I know that. I love you, too." She turned to shut the water off, and couldn't help the feeling of dread that overtook her. "Ty, it'll be fine. They'll get him, and then we won't have to be afraid anymore." She looked over her shoulder at him, but he still looked uneasy, making her feel cold and empty. What wasn't he telling her?

He opened the door to the shower, stepped out to get the towels, and wrapped one around her, patting her dry. He knew she was puzzled by his behavior, and hoped she would think it was because he was thinking of the business he had to take care of in L.A . "I'll call you when I land in L.A., and every morning before you leave for work." He hated lying to her, but she had to think that he would be in touch every day, or this plan would not work.

She giggled at that. "What, you're going to stay up until two or three in the morning, just to give me a wakeup call? That's nonsense, if you call me when you go to dinner, I'll be going to bed, so you can kiss me goodnight instead." She grinned cheekily at him.

He sighed, knowing he would be doing no such thing. "Good idea, then you can call me at lunch time to give me a wake-up call instead." He pulled her close again, saying goodbye and trying to keep his heart from breaking.

They hurriedly got dressed and ate breakfast. Maggie left for work, leaving Tyler to finish packing and wait for his driver. He could still change his mind, but he knew he wouldn't; if he did then Maggie wouldn't be safe. That was all that mattered, everything else would be fixed after the nut job was caught.

The weekend was quiet, but Maggie kept waiting for the next disaster to hit. Since Ty had left, there hadn't been any more phone calls. Maybe Tammy was right, and it was the two of them together that set the caller off. She'd talked to him only once since he left, although she wished he would call, she knew he was busy getting ready for the premiere of *Dragonfire*. She managed to get caught up on her household chores, and started making dough for Christmas cookies.

The TV was on to Entertainment Tonight© when Maggie entered the break room for dinner Monday evening. She stopped when she heard Ty's name, and looked up to the screen. There he was on the red carpet, with his arm wrapped around a beautiful blonde, Heidi Boyer. Both were smiling into the cameras, Ty saying that he was glad to have reconnected with Heidi, he'd missed her. When the reporter asked about the girl he had been dating in Pittsburgh, Tyler shrugged, said she was only a good friend, and helped both him and Heidi realize how much they meant to each other. Maggie was devastated; she had been unconsciously waiting for this to happen, but to hear it from his mouth was more than she could tolerate. She was suddenly glad that she'd not made a bigger fool of herself than she already had. She hadn't told anyone except Tammy about her feelings for Ty, any information came from his press conference after the hit-and-run incident. She looked furtively around the break room, and breathed a sigh of relief when she realized that she was alone. Maggie walked slowly over to the trash bin and dumped her uneaten dinner into the container. She poured a cup of coffee and just sat, staring at the wall for the next half hour.

On Wednesday, she saw the tabloids while standing in the cashier line at the grocery store. "Tyler and Heidi together again: Pittsburgh fling brought them closer together." Pictures of Ty and Heidi at the red carpet for *Dragonfire* took up the front page, while pictures of Maggie and Tyler were small inserts by the headline. She hoped that people around her didn't realize that she was the "Pittsburgh fling," and imagined pitying eyes on her. She hurriedly placed her items on the counter of the self-checkout to complete her purchases, trying to keep from bursting into tears. Once she reached the safety of her house, she allowed the tears to flow. Tammy phoned Maggie later in the evening, but she let the call go to voice mail, not having the energy to talk to anyone.

Thursday night at the Emergency Department was slow, and there was nothing to engage her thoughts, except images of the tabloids and the ET stories. Completing last minute preparations for the survey visit didn't really keep her mind occupied, she did the work by rote. Her thoughts kept drifting back to Tyler and how happy he seemed with Heidi; maybe the tabloids were right, he was just looking for a way to make Heidi jealous. Her heart told her that he'd been real and not using her, but she couldn't deny the evidence on E.T. How could he do this to her? She reminded herself that she had tried to prepare herself for this very event, but he was so persistent. She was such a fool! Her thoughts kept up a mantra of "Don't think about him" repeatedly until she thought she would scream.

Around two in the morning, the activity increased; the local chapter of the gun-and-knife club was out in full force. There were several bar fight victims, one with a knife sticking out of his chest. He kept trying to get off the cart to get to the man who put it in him. The second man only had minor injuries, and Casey Mitchell, the emergency department doctor, turned him over to the police once he was determined to be medically fit. The first man was taken to the operating room to have the knife removed. Although she knew she shouldn't be, Maggie was glad that there had been a bar fight to take her mind off her problems.

CHAPTER 19

No sooner were the rooms cleaned than the medic phone's annoying wail announced incoming trauma victims. A group of teens had been out partying, when their car went through a guardrail, flipping over. The driver wasn't wearing a seatbelt, and had been ejected; resuscitation efforts were underway. The four passengers were all in critical condition with varying injuries.

As the rest of the staff got the rooms ready, Maggie paged the trauma teams, anesthesia, and notified the blood bank. When she had finished with those calls, she called the Center for Organ Recovery and Education, to alert them of possible organ donors. She knew that some people would think that this was macabre, none of these kids were dead, and they may even recover completely, but Federal law mandated that C.O.R.E. be called for any impending death, and motor vehicle accidents were a cause for impending death. Especially when resuscitation efforts were being done for one of the victims who had been forcefully ejected from the vehicle. When the phone answered announcing she was on a recorded line, she identified herself and the hospital. She explained the accident, and asked that a coordinator come to the hospital to talk to the families. Once the calls were completed, she reviewed the preparations, then waited for the ambulances to arrive.

The trauma teams arrived just before the ambulances did, and David was part of the neurosurgical team. Just her luck, Maggie tried to avoid him by overstocking the supplies in the trauma rooms but he followed her.

"Maggie, I wanted to—"

Maggie cut him off. "Wanted to what? Gloat! Well, I'm fine, I knew what was going on and helped Tyler willingly. Save your comments for someone who needs them. Now go away, I'm busy. In case you've forgotten, we have incoming." She walked away, not looking back, and not seeing the confused expression on David's face.

He turned and walked back to the ambulance entrance. Maggie joined the teams a few minutes later, just as the first ambulance was pulling into the dock. The doors swung open and one of the medics jumped out.

The other medic was pushing the gurney out of the ambulance as Tony was helping to lower it to the ground, and started a brief report. "Hey, Maggie, Cindy Smith, nineteen, broken leg, head wound, and rib fractures. Vitals 102/56, pulse 128, respirations 30 and shallow. IV started LR, wide open."

Maggie directed him to Triage 9, and the thoracic trauma team followed behind. Tony turned to Maggie and said that it was a bad one, gave her a quick hug, and got back into the ambulance. As soon as they pulled out, the wail of a second ambulance announced their arrival.

The back flew open, and the two medics practically pushed the gurney out before it had completely stopped. The driver hurried over to guide the gurney to the ground.

As they pushed the gurney into the emergency department, Larry began his report. "This is the driver. Unrestrained, and ejected from the vehicle. Severe head injuries. Pupils two millimeters, equal, but sluggish. Was unconscious when we arrived and hasn't aroused. Probable internal bleeding as well, abdomen is rigid. We lost him once at the scene, and again in the ambulance. Intubated, with a seven-cuffed tube without difficulty. IVs wide open, this is the second bag."

Maggie called David's name, announcing that his patient had arrived. They swiftly moved to Trauma Room 1 and began assessing the damage to the young man.

The third ambulance pulled in with another female victim. She had been in the rear passenger seat, and had her seatbelt on. Her injuries were minor, mostly bruising from the seatbelt. She was crying and asking about Cindy. Maggie directed them to room 2 and waited for the last ambulance to arrive. The fourth ambulance drove up, and the medics brought the last patient in. He was unconscious, but had no obvious injuries. The medics report stated that he had been restrained, in the rear diver side of the vehicle, and was unconscious at the scene. Other than that, his vital signs were normal, and they could find no injuries, other than the seatbelt bruising, and the strong odor of alcohol. Maggie sent them to room 4 and followed them.

She had just finished sending the last patient to CT when she heard a keening scream from the waiting room. Maggie hurried out to the waiting room, already knowing what she would find. There were several people crowding the small area for trauma families, including the police. She looked around for any of the doctors and finding none, realized that it was not the terrible news of death that caused the woman's reaction, but the awareness that this was serious. The police officers saw Maggie and heaved a collective sigh, knowing she would help calm the woman where they couldn't.

Maggie sat down next to the sobbing woman, handing her a box tissues. "I'm Maggie, the charge nurse here. Will you tell me who you're waiting to hear about so I can get information for you?"

Maggie spoke in a soft, low voice, forcing the woman to stop crying so she could hear what Maggie was saying to her. The woman took a tissue, and began to swipe at her eyes.

"My son, the police said he was in a car accident, and was brought here. His name is Henry Dyle."

Maggie looked around the room to the others waiting. "Are you all families of the kids involved in the car accident?"

Each group nodded, and started to move toward Maggie.

"I'm sorry; I don't have any information for you, at the moment. We are still assessing each person, which will take a little while longer. As soon as I have any information, I'll be out to talk to all of you. In the meantime, is there anything I can get for you? There's coffee in the corner alcove, please help yourselves."

The police officers accompanied Maggie back to the nurses' station. "How are you, Maggie? Any news for us?" Al, the older officer, asked her.

She shook her head. "The driver is still in C.T., but I don't think he's going to make it. The others have severe injuries, I don't believe they're life threatening, but none of the tests are back yet."

"Dyle's the driver's name," Al told her. "It doesn't look like alcohol was involved for the driver; the medics didn't smell it on him. One of the others had alcohol on his breath, though."

They went back to the waiting room.

Maggie had already spoken to the Medical Examiner's office regarding Henry's impending death. Since the blood alcohol levels indicated that alcohol did not have a role in the accident, the M.E.'s office did not need to do an autopsy, and C.O.R.E. could have the body if the parents agreed.

Ron Brooks, the C.O.R.E. coordinator, arrived and spoke with the trauma doctors. Maggie's conclusion that Henry Dyle's injuries were too severe to survive were correct, the C.T. scan showed massive brain injury. David was going to speak to his parents, and Ron followed to discuss the possibility or organ donation. Maggie didn't envy either man's job, but went with them to offer support to Henry's mother.

David explained the extent of Henry's injuries to them.

"Henry has suffered a severe injury to his brain. The swelling was extreme. We have him on life support and can keep him on indefinitely, but with the extent of his injuries, it is unlikely that he will recover."

Maggie held on to Mrs. Dyle's hand while David explained this to them, then asked if she'd like to see Henry. Mrs. Dyle's tear-filled eyes found hers and she nodded. Maggie led them into the trauma room, all the while explaining what they would see, so they wouldn't be afraid. She stood behind Mrs. Dyle as she took her son's hand and kissed it. She patted his head and moved the hair from his forehead, telling him she loved him. She stayed that way for several minutes before she broke down again. Mr. Dyle put his arms around her, and gently led her out of the room. He looked at Maggie and in a somber voice asked about organ donation.

"Henry's older sister received a kidney transplant two years ago. It's what Henry would have wanted to do. His mother and I want to have part of him live on. What do we need to do?"

"Thank you. Whenever there's an accident like this, we are obligated to notify the organ donation center. Mr. Brooks is from the Center for Organ Recovery and Education. He's in the waiting room, and can explain the procedure for you, and answer any questions you have." She took them into one of the smaller, private rooms for families, and introduced Ron to them.

Maggie was drained, both physically and emotionally, while dealing with Henry's parents. They asked a many questions of both her and Ron. Mostly, they wanted to be reassured that he wasn't in pain now, and that by removing his organs and tissues they could have a funeral and viewing, to say their goodbyes. Ron assured them that would be possible. Mrs. Dyle took Maggie's hand, thanked her for caring for her son, and thanked Ron for his compassion, even while asking them to make this type of decision. Ron stepped forward, offered Mrs. Dyle his arm, and led her out of the hospital.

CHAPTER 20

The next several hours were still hectic. Each of the other accident victims were sent to surgery, and then to the Trauma Unit. The remaining families were torn between relief that their children would recover, and grief over Henry's death. After the last family member had been directed to the Trauma Unit to speak with the surgeons, Maggie and the rest of the staff started the cleaning and restocking of the trauma rooms. Housekeeping cleaned the floors and beds, while the nurses packaged the instruments to be sterilized and replaced them from the central stock. The work was monotonous and Maggie welcomed it. Nights like this were difficult to deal with.

Maggie appreciatively sank into a chair near the coffee pot, poured a cup, thanking whoever had made the fresh pot. She closed her eyes as she savored it, unaware that she wasn't alone, until David's voice shocked her eyes open.

"Maggie, you were wonderful with the Dyles. I never know how to talk to families like that."

"Thank you, David. I hear congratulations are in order. When is the baby due?"

"The beginning of March. And before you ask, no, Linda doesn't want to know the baby's sex." He sounded brusque, as if he didn't want to talk about the baby. "How are you, really, you look tired. I heard about that actor fellow. You really are too good for someone like him you know."

Maggie sat up straighter in her chair. "Thank you for your concern, if I look tired, it's because this has been a long and stressful shift. As for my private life, that's exactly what it is. Private."

"Maggie, wait! I didn't mean it that way. Look, I really need to talk to you but not here, not now. Will you have breakfast with me after shift?"

Maggie really looked at David for the first time since they broke up. He looked older somehow, his eyes were dull, and the smile he offered didn't reach them. "I'll let you know at end of shift, okay? I've got to get back." She got up, and taking her coffee with her, left the lounge. She would not cry, not here. Until David had spoken, she hadn't thought about Ty all night, and she wouldn't think about him now.

She finished charting and filing the reports regarding the organ donation, just as the day shift started streaming in. There were only two patients in the E.D., and the oncoming shift got report on them. Melissa and Cathy asked if Maggie wanted to have breakfast before they went home. Her first instinct was to refuse, but when they said they were going to Sommers Café, she agreed. They made the best chocolate-chip-pecan pancakes, and she was unexpectedly hungry. Besides, this way, she could avoid David's invitation.

The three of them caught up and laughed over chocolate-chip-pecan pancakes and bacon, orange juice, and coffee. She realized she missed this, the easy camaraderie of being with Melissa and Cathy after shift, with all the turmoil going on the past several weeks.

Melissa finally broached the subject of Tyler. "Maggie, do you want to talk about him?"

Maggie smiled, shaking her head. "There were things going on that I couldn't talk about at the time. I really am fine. I hope now things will get back to normal and that kook will stop bothering me."

Both friends looked dubious but didn't ask any more questions. They talked instead of the upcoming Christmas party that the E.D. doctors threw for the staff each year. This year was a black and white themed party. Cathy and Melissa were planning a shopping trip on Friday, since they were off, to find the perfect black and white dresses. Maggie listened and agreed albeit reluctantly, to accompany them, and look for something to wear. She wasn't sure she was in a Christmas Party mood but realized that if she made that comment, her friends would not let the subject of Ty alone.

They settled the bill and left the café. They were all off until tomorrow morning, Maggie was planning to sleep for a few hours, and then start baking the cookie dough she had stored in the refrigerator. Maggie's phone rang when she neared her street and she answered it automatically.

"Will you never learn? I told you to stay away, you have only yourself to blame for what has happened."

As she pulled onto her street, she found the road blocked with fire engines and police cars. She groaned and wondered what was going on now. A police officer waved her over and approached her car.

"Officer, I live on this street, my name's Maggie Jones."

The police officer asked her to get out of the car. Puzzled, she opened the door, asking what was wrong.

"Ms. Jones, there's been an incident...."

Nate walked toward them.

"Nate, what's going on? Why won't he let me go home?"

"Maggie, your garage burned, the preliminary investigation suggests arson." He saw the panic in her eyes and continued. "Taser's fine, he wasn't anywhere near the garage when it burned. In fact, his barking woke the neighbors, who called it in. Mr. Angolucci saw someone lurking around and called it in, but we didn't find anyone. That was around four o'clock. The fire alarm came in at four thirty. We figure it was a slow burn fuse and an accelerant."

Maggie let out a loud sigh. There wasn't much in the garage, just garden furniture and a lawn mower. She usually parked in the garage in bad weather, so she wouldn't have to scrape ice off the windshield. "Was anyone hurt?"

Nate shook his head.

"He called me just as I was pulling onto the street telling me I'd be sorry that I didn't stay away. Maybe this isn't related to Ty after all."

Nate looked thoughtful, and had Maggie repeat the phone call to him again. He agreed that maybe this was not related to Ty and the movie, but could offer no explanation. "Let's grab some things for you and you can crash at our place. The fire investigators will be here for a while yet."

Maggie nodded as Nate escorted her into her house to get clothes and toiletries. On the way out, Nate grabbed the container of dog food. Maggie was on autopilot as she followed Nate up the street to his house. Taser was in the front yard waiting for her, tail wagging furiously. She stooped to rub behind his ears and felt her face grow wet but not from Taser's tongue. Tears were streaming down her face. She was so tired and wanted this to be over. Nate touched her shoulder and helped her up; she swayed and found herself wrapped in Nate's arms. She sobbed against his chest, Taser nudged her elbow, and she placed one hand on his head. Nate gently led her into the house and up to the guest room. Maggie crawled onto the bed with Taser lying on the floor next to her. He looked at Nate as if to say, "It's all under control, I'm watching over her." Nate scratched his ears and closed the door softly as he left.

Maggie slept until five o'clock. When she woke, Tammy was in the kitchen, and Nate had already left for his shift. They sat at the table as Tammy filled her in on the arson investigation. The police and arson investigator would be prowling around for a few more days, but since the garage was a totally separate building, Maggie would be permitted back into her house whenever she wanted. She opted to spend the night with Tammy and go home in the morning.

Because of Maggie's previous association with Ty, the story of her garage burning down was an item on Entertainment Tonight. Maggie missed the story because she was lounging in the Jacuzzi tub on the back deck, trying to chill. She also missed the phone call Tyler made to Tammy asking how she was.

"Ty, I know you thought your leaving would get this nut-job to back off. Maggie got a call on her way home from work saying that she hadn't learned to stay away from him. I guess we were both wrong and the 'him' isn't you. How's Heidi handling all the publicity and drama?"

"Good, the premiere was fun. She knows the drill; she and I date each other for the tabloids and paparazzi. We help each other out that way, I cover for her, and she pretends to be the understanding girlfriend, who overlooks my wandering eye. I thought that if the stalker believed that I wasn't interested in Maggie, then he'd quit bothering her. I gather that isn't the case any longer. Any ideas on what is going on? Who is calling her?"

"I don't know, Ty. When the calls started, we all assumed that it was because of you and the movie, the timing was right. Now I just don't know, we'll have to start over, see if there's anything we missed because we were concentrating on your connection to Maggie." Tammy thought over what Ty had said or rather not said. "Tyler, what do you mean you cover for Heidi by being her escort? I thought Hollywood didn't frown on alternative lifestyles anymore."

He sighed. "They don't usually. We've been friends for a long time, no one else knows except Katie, her partner. Katie's okay with it, she doesn't want to be in the spotlight. She and Heidi have been together since college. But Heidi is in the running for the lead in a TV series, the sponsors would not look favorably on her lifestyle. Heidi's a good actress, and she will rock in this part. We'll be breaking up again, once she gets signed. Please, just believe me, I. LOVE. MAGGIE."

"All right, I'll be interested in hearing all the details when I see you. Your plan didn't work too well, though, he's still after her. Maybe we're looking at this the wrong way. I have the feeling I'm missing something, I just don't know what."

They talked for a few more minutes, as Tyler said goodbye, he asked Tammy keep Maggie safe.

Tammy wasn't sure she should say anything to Maggie about Ty's phone call. She knew that seeing him with Heidi had upset her; she saw how Maggie had slunk back inside herself. Hearing Ty's side of it, she realized just how much he loved Maggie and wanted to keep her safe, but thought he was going about it the wrong way in light of the new incident. The nagging feeling that she was missing an important piece of the puzzle kept at her.

Maggie came back into the house just then, wrapped in her hot pink terrycloth robe. Her skin was flushed from the hot tub and she looked more relaxed. Tammy made up her mind to wait until later to tell Maggie about Ty's call, she didn't want to undo the benefits of the hot tub. They both went to bed shortly after that, and Maggie slept straight through feeling refreshed, when she woke the next morning. Maggie insisted on returning to her house after breakfast, and the police and arson investigators just reinforced that she and Taser stay out of the backyard and the area around the garage. That was not going to be difficult, she wanted nothing to do with any reminders of the stalker.

After she changed and packed Taser's food, they walked slowly down the street to her home. She was relieved when she saw the police car in front. and stopped to talk to the officer in the driver's seat. Since this was not the first attack on her, the police were keeping a close eye on her. She knew that the likelihood of the stalker returning was slim since there was a marked police car in front of her house blocking the driveway, but there was that part of her that remembered the cheesy horror-slasher movies that had the murderer getting past the parked police car and attacking the female lead anyway. She shook off that thought, smiling at the thought of her as a leading lady, and entered the comforting silence of the house. She locked the door and set the alarm, heading into the kitchen to make a cup of tea. She absently poured kibble into Taser's bowl and took the teapot out of the cupboard.

Maggie was comfortably numb as she made her tea and sat in her kitchen, listening to the house creak in the stillness. As she savored the tea, her thoughts wandered to what had happened since October's freak snowstorm. Some of it had been wonderful, some scary, and finally, some downright heartbreaking. She realized that she wouldn't have traded any of it, her time with Tyler had been spectacular and she would keep it in her heart forever. She smiled ruefully, as she got up to rinse her cup, when the window shattered, spraying glass everywhere. The blaring of the glass break alarm shattered the quiet, while something hot scraped against her arm. Maggie spun around and ran to fling open the front door for the officers. One came into the house talking on the radio to his partner who was at the back of the house.

"There's fresh footprints back here, Mac. Nothing else. Maggie okay?"

Mac looked over at her, and she smiled weakly at him.

"I'm okay, Mac."

She saw him looking at her arm and glanced at it to see blood dripping down her sleeve. Oh, that's what the burning was, a bullet, has to be here somewhere. She moved her arm to show where she had been standing, and realized that if she hadn't stood when she had, the bullet would have hit her in the head.

Maggie paled and sank into the chair. "I was sitting here, just a moment before the window broke. I could have been killed!"

Once the police and medics left, Maggie having convinced the medics that she was fine and just needed cleaned and bandaged, she sat in the kitchen with Taser. Her head hurt from trying to figure out what was going on, why was she still being targeted? Tyler was back in L.A. with Heidi. She was so tired and just wanted to be left alone. She didn't know how long she sat there, but the light through the kitchen window was fading, when she finally shook herself and got up. Taser jumped up from under her chair and headed toward his bowl. He looked reproachfully at her for forgetting about his dinner as he pawed the dish. She scratched his head and opened the food bin, scooping kibble into his bowl.

"I'm sorry, baby. I didn't mean to forget about your dinner."

Taser licked her hand as if in forgiveness, and set his attention to eating. The thought of food was anathema to her, but she made herself a sandwich and ate it absently, while getting the cookie dough out of the fridge. She knew she had to keep busy so she wouldn't have time to think about anything, except the task at hand.

With the first batch baking, Maggie finished her meal, and washed up the small amount of dishes by hand. She got out the sprinkles and frosting for the sugar cookie cutouts, just as the oven timer went off. She slid the next tray into the oven and she concentrated on decorating the cookies when they cooled enough. She had the radio on to the "all Christmas music until Christmas" station and hummed with the music. She felt the tension drain out of her body, as she decorated the cookies and placed them on trays. Her assembly line style of baking kept her busy, until she had the last roll of dough cut out, baked, and decorated. She looked at the clock, it was almost midnight, and no wonder she was tired. She placed some of the cookies on a plate and took them out to the officers standing watch over her house along with a thermos of coffee. They thanked her, and wished her a good-night. She smiled at them, and turned back to the house and bed. Her sleep was undisturbed and Maggie headed to work the next morning feeling better than she had in a while.

CHAPTER 21

The mood only lasted until lunchtime. David was in the cafeteria line when she went to lunch, when he spotted Maggie, he moved to her side.

"Please, I'd like to talk to you. May I join you?"

Maggie frowned at him as she picked up her tray and utensils. She walked quickly to the salad bar, and began making her plate.

"Maggie, please. I want to clear the air between us. I've been thinking a lot since I talked to you last week." He made to take her arm but evidently thought better of it, pulling back.

Maggie stared into his face for a few seconds, and finally nodded. "Okay, you can have lunch with me." She finished making her salad, and moved to the refrigerated section, to grab a bottle of water with David hurrying to catch up.

They moved to the checkout line, and soon found a table near the windows overlooking the outdoor smoking area.

"Thank you, Maggie. I know I treated you badly but I need to explain."

"Explain!? What could you possibly have to explain, except you slept with my roommate while we were dating and got her pregnant! The entire surgical staff knew about it before I did." She felt herself become more agitated, and forced several deep breaths to calm herself. "Look, just say whatever it is you want to say and then leave me the hell alone. Permanently."

David gazed at her before he began. "I didn't know anyone when I ran into you. You seemed so nice, and I liked how you smiled at me, when you told me how to get to the call rooms. After we started dating, I met Linda when we were both on call. We talked for a while; I didn't know she was your roommate then. And she didn't know I had been dating you, and started talking about different couples. She mentioned that you and Sebastian were an item. You never said you were dating anyone else, I thought from your conversations that you were unattached, and here, you're involved with the Chief of Transplant Surgery! I was angry and hurt. The next morning, I saw you talking to him and he hugged you. When Linda asked me to have breakfast with her, I went. She was funny, and I was attracted to her. We never said we were exclusive, and I went out with her when you were working late. The night you came home, that was when I realized that she lived with you, we'd always gone out or to my place. She opened the door when I pulled up. One thing led to another, and Linda told me she was pregnant, I wanted to do the right thing. We got married over Labor Day weekend in Las Vegas."

The more he talked, the angrier Maggie became. Linda knew she was dating David; she had been in the kitchen once when he came to pick her up on. She almost didn't hear what he said next.

"I found out that I'm not the father, Stan, one of the surgical techs is. I told her I want a divorce. I'm not telling you this to try to get you back; I know I messed that up too badly. I just want you to know how sorry I am that I listened to her in the first place. I heard that Sebastian is getting married, I'm sorry. Will you forgive me, at least to the point that we can talk when we have to work together?"

"David, I'm sorry about the baby, I know how excited you were. Linda lied about a lot of things. Sebastian is a good friend; his sister Beth, Tammy, and I were best friends from first grade, until she died her Freshman year at Pitt. The day you saw him hug me, at work, was the anniversary of her death. We both were a little teary that day. I know he's getting married, I'm in the wedding. He's marrying Samantha, one of our CORE liaisons, I introduced them. I accept that we have to work together, but don't ask any more of me. I'm glad we could clear the air. But for now, please, just keep your distance." Maggie picked up the remnants of her lunch and left the cafeteria.

Just what she didn't need, hearing that Linda was as manipulative in her marriage as she had been in her friendships. She knew Linda had been playing the field when she made her move on David, but she honestly thought she had settled down. Did Stan know she was pregnant with his child, and passing it off as David's, she wondered? It wasn't her problem and she smiled to herself, thinking she'd like to be around when this came out. She headed to the E.D. in better spirits than she had been since she saw David in the cafeteria.

She entered the locker room to find Linda sitting on the bench, her good mood vanished. "Linda, what are you doing here, are you all right?"

Linda looked up and smiled at her. Her face was drawn and she sported a black eye. "What happened to your face?"

"I'm okay, it looks worse than it is. I slipped and fell on the ice is all. My balance is off with the baby. I just wanted to see you; I heard what's been happening, and wanted to make sure you were okay. We used to be friends, and I, um, well that's all." She stood up awkwardly, her pregnancy made her off balance. "David said you were holding up well. You always were strong, nothing affects you."

"Is that what you think? It just doesn't serve any purpose to wring my hands and cry about it. That won't change what is going on." Maggie tried not to sound bitter. She wondered what Linda's true motive was; they hadn't talked since Linda moved out of her house. Linda gave a strangled laugh and said she could think of several men who would love to comfort her, including David.

It was Maggie's turn to laugh, she wasn't about to let her know what David had confided to her over lunch. "Linda, David stays as far away from me as he can, after I threatened to emasculate him for sleeping with you while we were together. I don't think he'd be too anxious to offer me comfort. Is that why you're here, Linda, to see if David has been consoling me? Your pregnancy hormones are going haywire. We talk to each other only when he has a patient here in the E.D. Now, if you'll excuse me, I have to get back to work. I hope you have a healthy baby."

Maggie walked toward her locker, aware that Linda was staring after her. When Maggie had finished hanging her lab coat, she turned to see that Linda had silently left. She shook her head, heaving a sigh of relief, and headed out to the main E.D.

CHAPTER 22

The movie crew was making progress, mainly, because the weather was holding. There had been no more mishaps since the crane and lighting rig had crashed. Sal was hoping to wrap the film within the next three days. Tyler would be back tomorrow, and the last scenes would be completed then. Today, the schedule was concentrating on Peter Soffel's hastily cleaning of the Biddle brothers cell at the jail, and meeting his mistress to arrange a meeting in Ohio the next month. The final scene would be Peter's resignation speech upon hearing of Kate's being wounded and captured in Butler. The rehearsal went smoothly; Tim Hicks was on his marks and his ad lib speech interjections added to the portrayed misery and betrayal. Sal called for positions and camera set up. The assistant director updated the clapboard, and the cameraman began rolling tape.

"Action!" Sal called out, and Tim stepped up to the podium and began to speak. "In one way, I would like to stay here—if the whole three are captured alive. I would like to see them brought back, and placed under my care. I say oh, but I wish that could happen. I tell you the revenge I would take would be sweet."

As soon as he began the second part of his statement, that he had been under the effects of chloroform during the escape, most likely administered by his wife; the lectern suddenly exploded, bursting into flames quickly igniting Tim's clothing. Time seemed to stop, then people began to run toward the flames. One of the extras whipped off his coat and wrapped Tim in it, pulling him down to the ground, and rolling him over. Others grabbed the fire extinguishers and smothered the lectern's flames.

Tim was moaning, and the man, who had helped put out his flames, kept him down until the ambulance arrived. After Tim had been loaded into the ambulance and taken to the hospital, the arson squad asked Sal to send the crew to the meal tent except for the "Good Samaritan." The Samaritan's name was Lee Armstrong, a local man, who answered the ad for extras on the movie set as a reporter. He was a personal trainer at the South Side Works, but had the day off. As a trainer, he had first aid classes and just reacted to Tim's screams. The police let him leave after a few questions and fixed their attention on the smoldering lectern.

They found the remains of a cell phone, attached to wires leading to a glass container that smelled of kerosene. The fire was definitely arson, and since neither Maggie nor Ty was involved with today's filming, the movie was definitely the target this time. Jacob arrived and spoke to the crime scene investigators about the bomb remnants. He watched as they bagged evidence, and put the bomb parts into sealable cans. It would take a while to get anything from all that stuff.

The movie crew hadn't moved, they knew the routine, and were waiting for Jacob and the other police officers and detectives to gather their statements. Sal had them move to the catering tent, watching as they moved silently toward empty chairs. Jacob moved into the center of the room making eye contact with as many members of the crew as he could.

"I know you are familiar with the questioning by now. Those of you crewmembers, who were part of the scene setup, please go to the right side of the tent to discuss the day's events with me. The extras who were part of the scene, please move to the left side of the tent with Sgt. Hawthorne. Those of you who were not directly involved with today's shooting schedule, please go with Detective Stewart to make sure we have your contact information and fingerprints on file."

The groups formed as directed and moved to various parts of the tent.

Jacob looked up in time to see Nick DiMarco trying to squeeze out through a back opening. He moved quickly to intercept him, and managed to grab an arm. "Nice try, DiMarco. Let's have a talk downtown. You're under arrest for the bombing and attempted murder of Tim Hicks. You have the right to remain silent…."

Jacob finished the Miranda Rights as they moved toward the squad car. The rest of the movie crew began to move away, and the police officers allowed them to leave.

Once at the police station, Nick waived his right to an attorney. "I didn't do nothin'. I was trying to get out of there, 'coz I knew you'd pin this on me." He looked defiantly at Jacob.

"Then you won't mind if we swab your hands for explosive residue, will you?" He motioned for the lab tech to swab Nick's hands.

Nick crossed his arms and glared at the lab tech. "On second thought, I want a lawyer. I'm done talking."

"I thought that's what you would say."

Jacob left the room with the lab tech, allowing Nick to stew for a while. Forty minutes later Nick made his phone call to the public defender's office. An attorney would be there within an hour, he was advised not to talk to the police until the attorney arrived. Nick was led back to a holding cell to wait for the lawyer. Jacob called the lab tech to swab the phone for transfer residue from Nick's hand. The results came back positive; Jacob collected the evidence and headed toward the interrogation room.

The Public Defender arrived, and spent time reviewing the charges and speaking with Nick. When Jacob entered the room, the lawyer began immediately by saying, "There is no basis for the charges against my client. Your evidence is circumstantial at best, you found him leaving a scene of an accident, and there is no connection between my client and the explosion."

"Well, Ms. Myers, as it happens, there is a connection between your client and the explosion. We found explosive residue on your client's hands. The residue matches the explosives we found at the scene. And, before you ask, no, we didn't violate your client's rights, we simply swabbed the phone he used to call you. All perfectly legal, I assure you since the phone is public domain." Jacob sat and waited for the information to set in. He didn't have long to wait.

"Detective, may I have a few minutes with my client to go over this new information?"

Jacob graciously acceded and left the room for a cup of coffee. He walked down the hall to Tammy's office and informed her of the latest development. "So, I'm headed back to see what kind of deal Nick wants to make. You can let Maggie know that we caught him, so she's safe. It'll be a great Christmas for her." Jacob left the room and returned to the interrogation room.

When Jacob entered the room, Olivia Myers took a deep breath.

"What are you offering?"

"Who said anything about a deal, Ms. Myers?"

"Detective, you wouldn't have told us about the explosive residue if you weren't planning to offer a deal. So let's have it."

"Any deal on the table is contingent on your client telling me everything about the attacks on the movie, the actors and crew, and Ms. Jones. Then we'll talk deal."

Olivia looked at Nick, who nodded, and he began to talk. "They shouldn't be making that movie. She was an evil woman, and don't deserve to be heroic. She was nothin' but trash. Running around with those killers, and leaving her kids like that. No one was supposed to get hurt; I just wanted to stop the movie."

Jacob listened to Nick's confession and wondered how Maggie and Tyler fit in to the picture; Nick hadn't mentioned them yet.

"I didn't know the crane would fall, or the lights, I just wanted to short them out. And the bomb under the podium, it shouldn't have set Tim on fire like that. The laxative in the chicken was okay, no one got hurt with that, the other things just were worse than I wanted. You can't blame me for things not working the way they should."

Nick continued to rant about the movie, and how it must be stopped. Jacob interrupted and asked him about the abduction of Tyler Sinclair.

"We weren't going to hurt him, just keep him unavailable for a few days. The weather got in the way, and then he jumped out of the car when it got stuck."

"What about the attacks on Maggie Jones?"

"Maggie's a decent person, she shouldn't have gotten involved with Sinclair. I just wanted to stop the movie. They were trying to make Peter look like he was involved, so he could dump Kate. That's just not right."

The rest of the story came out; Nick was a descendent of one of Kate's children. He knew the story, and how it tore Peter and the children apart. Peter had been faithful to Kate but the scandal of her helping the Biddles escape, and run off with them, was too much to deal with. They shouldn't make a movie about Peter being the one to suggest to Kate that she befriend the brothers, and make it easy for her to help them escape, so he could get rid of her.

His ranting continued until Jacob asked, "Was Sandi involved with any of this?"

Nick looked startled, as if he forgot where he was, "Yeah, she helped dose the chicken. I convinced her it was a joke. But she didn't do anything else."

Ms. Myers looked at Jacob, and asked softly if there would be a deal.

Jacob nodded but added, "It depends on how Mr. Hicks does. The burns are pretty bad, if he dies, then I can't offer a deal, it'll be Murder One then."

Myers closed her eyes, "I know. However, listening to him rant, I think I need to seek psychiatric help for him. I'll be in touch." She shook Jacob's hand, and put her hand on Nick's shoulder to arouse him.

He looked around the room, as he was led back to his cell. "I'm sorry, I didn't mean for anyone to get hurt."

Jacob sat in the interrogation room for a few minutes, mulling over the last three quarters of an hour. He shook his head, and left the room. Now that DiMarco was behind bars, the movie crew would be able to wrap up, and most of them would be home for Christmas. He called Maggie to let her know.

"Maggie, it's over. Nick DiMarco was behind all of the incidents on the movie set. He confessed. Of course, his lawyer is going to pursue a psychiatric defense; he was pretty out there, ranting about how Kate shouldn't be glorified. He's related distantly to Kate's children. He didn't like the fact that the movie portrayed Peter as the mastermind behind the escape to get rid of Kate, without looking like the bad guy. He's grown up hearing the story, and how Kate was the one who cheated, and helped two convicted murderers escape justice. Seeing Kate made out to be a victim was too much for him. There's a press conference in half-an-hour to announce it. Merry Christmas, honey."

Maggie hung up from Jacob's call, and looked around, then at the calendar. It was December 20; she needed to get moving on decorating and cooking. She felt energized, and more relaxed than she had in weeks. The tree was already in the front room, waiting for the decorations to adorn it; it was an artificial one, but perfectly shaped and lit. She loved the smell of fresh pine, but wasn't home long enough to make sure a real tree stayed watered. She compensated by decorating the mantles with live pine boughs, so the scent would permeate the space, she'd pick them up on her way home from work tomorrow. For now, she opened the boxes of ornaments and began to gently wipe each one, as she removed it from its protective wrapping. Almost all of them were hand-blown glass from Germany, dating from before World Wars I and II. Each year, her grandparents, and then her parents had added to the collection; there were wax Santas, angels, and toy soldiers, Snow White and the Dwarfs made of pinecones, glass ornaments with various scenes inside: the Nativity, shepherds, magi, and angels, satellites and stars from the sixties, and then the ones she purchased when she started to work. Each one was precious, because of the history behind them. She had a hard time each year deciding which ones would be in the front. She worked tirelessly on the tree for several hours until it finally met with her approval. She folded the ladder and turned the power on to light the tree. The soft light illuminated the window and she smiled at the result. Taser nudged her, now that the lights were on, to remind her it was well past his dinnertime.

They made their way into the kitchen, Maggie placed kibble into Taser's bowl, and began to look for something quick for dinner for herself. She took a container of soup out of the freezer and placed it into the microwave. While it was warming, she fixed a cup of tea, and went back into the front room to admire the tree.

After eating the soup and showering, Maggie crawled sleepily into bed. She was looking forward to returning to a normal life. As she began to drift into sleep, thoughts of Ty came unbidden and she sighed. "Well, almost normal, I suppose. I haven't thought about him all day. I'm getting better." She smiled to herself and fell into a deep, dreamless sleep.

CHAPTER 23

Christmas was a quiet affair, Maggie spent Christmas Eve with Nate and Tammy's family, then accompanied them to Midnight Service. She went to work on Christmas Day to a tranquil Emergency Department. It seemed as if everyone was celebrating the holiday spirit by staying home and healthy. She brought food in for lunch and dinner for the E.D. team and knew word would spread that she had cooked. People would begin to crawl out of the woodwork around mealtime to mooch, she didn't mind, there was always plenty of food to go around. At roughly eleven, the phone rang and Melissa held the receiver to her shrugging her shoulders.

"This is Maggie, how can I help you?"

"Merry Christmas, beautiful. Don't hang up, please." Ty's voice was anxious.

"What do you want?" Maggie said tersely, she was tempted to hang up, but she simply wanted to hear his voice too much. She felt her heart begin to race, vexed by the fact that she was glad he had called. "How did you know I'd be here?"

"Well, I did try your house first, and when you didn't answer, I knew you probably volunteered to work. I really want to talk to you, in fact, I need to explain what has been in the tabloids. I'd do it now but, I'd rather do it face-to-face. I'm flying into Pittsburgh the day after New Year's," he trailed off expectantly.

Maggie didn't answer for a few seconds, trying to get her emotions under control. She wasn't sure she could face seeing him. The stories in the tabloids and on ET left her vulnerable, and she was still hurting. "Do we have things to talk about? I'm not sure we do, Ty." Maggie struggled not to cry, hearing his voice, and remembering the cabin, and his slow passionate lovemaking. Did she want to see him? She couldn't lie to herself about her feelings for him. She made up her mind, she wanted to see him. "I'm working the split shift this week, but I'll be off New Year's Day and the day after. I'm not sure if I want to talk to you, let alone see you, to be honest. Can I call you to let you know?" She knew she'd have to be well prepared for this encounter.

"Of course, I understand. I hope you can fit me into your schedule. I miss you, Maggie; I love you. I know you most likely don't believe me, considering the tabloids and the paparazzi. Things aren't what they seem, and I want to explain everything, just give me a chance." He sounded so sincere, had he really missed her? She would think about it and call him after the New Year.

She had too much time to think. The rest of the day was slow, only a few patients to care for and most weren't admitted. At three o'clock, distraught parents came flying into the automatic doors, with a cute blond-haired, three-year-old boy choking in the mother's arms. Chad received a Lego® set for Christmas and, since everything went into his mouth, he attempted to swallow a piece. Only problem, the Lego® was larger than Chad's throat. It lodged there and Chad had been choking since. Maggie took him, and the parents, into one of the treatment rooms and placed a face tent over Chad's face with oxygen. Alan came in and spoke to the parents while Maggie started an IV in Chad's arm. He was so worn out from choking, that he barely moved when she inserted the needle. She hung a bag of fluid, and assembled the necessary equipment to remove the Lego® and waited for Alan to finish his discussion. Alan explained that he would administer a numbing medication to the back of Chad's throat, and what he would do step-by-step to remove the Lego®. In actuality, it took longer to explain than it did to remove it.

Chad was fine, but stayed in the E.D. for almost an hour, until the numbness wore off and his breathing was normal. Alan gave Chad the Lego® piece and made him promise not to swallow any more Lego® pieces. The parents left, and the E.D. went back to having no patients, but plenty of well-fed staff members. The staff were eating in shifts and having a good time in the break room, when Chad's parents came back to the E.D.

Sarah came back to the break room to let Maggie know they were back. She and Alan looked at each other and shrugged. "So much for not sticking Lego® pieces in his mouth. I'll get the room set up while you bring them back, okay, Maggie?"

Maggie nodded and went to get them.

"Dr. Alan, I didn't swallow the Lego®, Daddy did!" Chad called out when they came into the exam room.

Alan looked up at the trio, listening to the partially obstructed breathing of Chad's dad. "Have a seat; you know what I'm going to do."

Alan sprayed Dad's throat and reached back with the tonsillar forceps to pull out the Lego® piece. He handed the piece to Chad and told him not to let Dad play with them. Chad, Sr.'s voice was hoarse.

"I was trying to see how he could have got the piece stuck. It's slippery and just slid into my throat."

Chad giggled, and put the piece in his pocket. Maggie gave them discharge instructions once the numbness wore off, told them if either had difficulty breathing, to come back immediately, and sent them home.

The rest of the evening was uneventful, and Maggie went home at eleven-thirty. She was still chuckling about Chad's dad and the Lego® pieces. She fixed a cup of tea and sat in the front room, relaxing to the lights of the tree. Taser curled up at her feet and snored softly. She allowed herself to think about Ty's phone call. She wanted to see him. She still loved him. She wasn't sure she could face him. He said he needed to talk to her face-to-face, and that the tabloids don't always tell the whole story. What could he want to discuss, other than he was really in-volved with Heidi? She was giving herself a headache, thinking about this. She would put all this out of her mind until New Year's, and then decide if she would see Ty or not. She could wait until then to call him. Having made her decision, she rinsed her cup and headed to bed.

CHAPTER 24

"I hate New Year's Eve, it's depressing. What is so great about the end of a year, you're just another year older, with nothing to show for it." Maggie faced Tammy. "I'm not going anywhere tonight. We have this argument every year, so why should this year be any different?"

Tammy shook her head. "I think you should change things beginning, with New Year's Eve; go with us. We're only going to the James Street Tavern for a meal, some jazz and a few drinks, come with us." She knew that Maggie never went out on New Year's Eve, but this year she had to get her to go with them, if only to take her mind off everything that had been going on. Now that Nick DiMarco was in custody, she hoped that Maggie was no longer in danger. "Maggie, you have to get out. You've done nothing but go to work and come home. I don't even see you waking at the field anymore. This cannot go on; you have to either talk to him or let it go." Maggie only glared at Tammy, not bothering to hide her disgust.

"I'm fine. I've been out, the groceries are fresh, and Taser and I have walked the field every morning. You know that I've never been much for clubbing. Now why don't you, Nate, and Jacob just go and enjoy yourselves? I have a lot to do this evening."

Tammy rolled her eyes, noting that Maggie didn't comment on her remark about getting over Ty. "Doing what?"

Maggie shook her head. "Laundry for one, I'm out of scrubs and underwear. If I don't do it tonight, I won't have anything to wear to work tomorrow morning." She moved toward the door, hoping Tammy would get the message and leave.

"I did that for you already, I knew you'd try to get out of going with us tonight with that excuse. Besides, I know you aren't scheduled tomorrow, so you don't really need the laundry done tonight. Now, go get showered and dressed, I'll wait here for you."

Maggie didn't have another excuse. She gave in reluctantly. "You don't have to wait, I'll meet you there."

"We'll wait dinner for you, but if you aren't there in an hour, I'm coming back to get you."

With that, Tammy pushed Maggie toward the stairs, listening as Maggie muttered something about police brutality. Forty minutes later, freshly showered, Maggie her hair dried, applied a little makeup, and slipped into a dark green dress. As she pushed into the matching pumps, the doorbell rang.

"Geez, it's only been forty-five minutes Tammy, get a grip." Maggie hurried down the stairs and pulled open the door.

"Hello, Maggie, I think we need to continue our chat from the other day. May I come in?"

The unwelcomed guest didn't wait for an invitation, but pushed in and sauntered into the living room.

"Close the door, Maggie, and have a seat. There is so much more we need to talk about. I see you were able to replace the door's window. I felt badly about breaking that antique stained glass, but I needed to make sure I had your full attention."

Maggie tried to hide her shock at the words. "Linda, I just on my way out to meet Tammy and Nate. I'm sure there really isn't anything we need to discuss." Maggie stayed by the open door, hoping Linda would take the hint.

Linda looked ill, her eyes were overly bright, but her skin was pale, with a light sheen of sweat on her forehead.

"Are you all right? You look ill." Maggie was beginning to become alarmed, something was off, and she wasn't sure what it was.

Linda laughed, a high-pitched cackle, and moved toward Maggie. "I look ill! You, better than anyone, knows why that is. I've seen the two of you, plotting against me. That ploy with the actor, to make him jealous worked, he hated seeing you with someone else. I thought you were so mousey and stupid; I underestimated you. You've been trying to get him back since we got married. How did you find out about the baby? I was so careful to make David believe it was his and you told him. Now he wants to divorce me, and I'll have nothing, no money, no status as an up-and-coming neurosurgeon's wife, and some brat that I don't even want!" She railed at Maggie, her voice rising as she finished her rant.

Maggie tried to calm her. "Linda, I didn't know any of this, I swear. I haven't been talking to David, except in the E.D., I told you that. He stopped me for lunch the other day, and when he started talking about you and the baby, I left." Maggie hoped she could convince Linda that she didn't know about the baby and the divorce. "I told him I wanted nothing to do with him, and unless a patient was involved, not to seek me out or talk to me. We're done; I wouldn't take him back if you gave him to me on a platter."

Linda gaped at her and sneered. "You wouldn't take him back on a platter!" She scoffed, "Even after that actor dumped you! Isn't David good enough?"

"Linda, he doesn't want me, he loves you. Let me call him so he can tell you himself. You really look ill, Linda. Let me get him for you so he can take care of you." Maggie pleaded, trying to convince Linda to back away.

Linda moved close enough that Maggie could smell the alcohol on her breath. "I LOVE him, no one else. I made a mistake about the baby, not telling him. I thought he would never find out." She eyed Maggie maliciously, and pulled the revolver out of the pocket of her jacket. "Why did you have to ruin everything and tell him? How did YOU find out? He looks for you at the hospital. He calls your name in his sleep. You took him away from me, and you don't even want him!" Linda's eyes glazed over, she moved swiftly toward Maggie. "The only way to keep him is to get rid of you forever."

Taser chose that time to wander in from the kitchen. On sensing how tense Maggie was, he started to growl low in his throat. Linda was distracted, shifting her gaze to the snarling German Sheppard; Maggie realized that this would be her only chance. She bolted out the door, feeling something slam into her a second before she heard the retort of the revolver. She took a few more steps, and had the feeling of being pushed forward, with a second flash of heat, as her body became heavy, and the sound of another gunshot rang through the night.

As she fell forward, she heard the third shot, and struggled to get off the ground. The sound jolted Maggie, and she turned back to the front door calling for Taser, suddenly afraid that the third shot was aimed at him. Maggie was trying to crawl through a dark tunnel that kept closing in on her; her hand hit the steps, and she collapsed, unable to lift her arms or legs to climb them. The sound of a car door slamming, and Tammy's voice calling her name, made her turn her head to see footsteps running toward her. She thought of Tyler, sadly wanting to kiss him one more time, then darkness enveloped her.

CHAPTER 25

Pain, Maggie's world was filled with it, she tried to move, but her body wouldn't respond. She strained to make sense of what was happening to her, but it was too hard to think with the pain. Darkness shrouded her, and there was no more pain, it didn't last, though. Through the haze of pain, she heard voices, fragments of conversations that she was sure was about her.

"How badly is she hurt, Doctor?" That was Tammy's voice filled with distress and fear.

"The bullet missed her spine, I was able to remove it without much difficulty. There shouldn't be any permanent damage. The second bullet shattered the femur. That is going to take a months of physical therapy to heal. There was a great deal of muscle damage; I'm not sure if the leg will be able to withstand the strain of floor work. She was very lucky she didn't lose that leg." Lucky! He wasn't the one lying here in pain. The welcomed darkness engulfed her again.

"Well, she said she didn't want to go out for New Year's, but this was a little over the top, even for her!"

Jacob's voice, was laughing at her, trying to ease the tension in the room. She supposed it was funny; she did get out of celebrating New Year's Eve, but she ruined it for them as well. She tried to move her hand to slap him for making fun of her, but still couldn't get her body to respond. Was the doctor wrong, was she paralyzed? No, it must be the after-effects of the anesthesia and pain medication. She felt the darkness creep in again, permitting herself to succumb to it.

Maggie became aware of the noises surrounding her, the steady beep, beep, beep of the cardiac monitor. She listened to the rhythm and smiled, it sounded normal. She heard more sounds as she slowly aroused, the soft thrumming of the IV pump, the sounds of the creaking chairs, her breathing, and the sounds of soft snoring to her left. She turned her head, and was surprised and pleased, that this time, her body responded. Nate was sitting in the chair next to her bed, sleeping. Tammy was on the sofa by the window, but her eyes were focused on Maggie. When she saw that Maggie was awake, she hurried over to her.

"Hey, there. I'm so glad you're awake; we were all so worried." Maggie could hear the strain in her voice as Tammy tried to keep control.

Maggie nodded slowly. "You've been here the whole time, I could hear you talking, but I couldn't answer you. How long?"

"It's Wednesday morning. You missed New Year's Eve, and New Year's Day. We took turns staying, and going to look in on Taser."

"Taser, did she shoot him, too, I heard another shot!" Maggie tried to sit up, groaned in pain, and fell back onto the bed.

"No, she didn't shoot Taser, he's fine. We were there a while ago to feed and walk him. He misses you; he keeps going to the steps, pawing at them."

"Then she tried to shoot me a third time?" Maggie looked up at Tammy. "Twice wasn't enough for her?"

"She shot herself, Maggie."

Maggie was aghast. "She shot herself! Is she...." Maggie trailed off.

"No—at least not yet. They aren't sure she'll make it. She shot herself in the abdomen, lost the baby, and a lot of blood. She's in bad shape. There is evidence of drug use too. Narcotics and cocaine. She's been unconscious since the medics brought her in."

"She was desperate to keep David from divorcing her. The baby wasn't his, I suppose she thought if it weren't there any more, he would stay married to her. She really was sick when she came to see me, mentally and physically. What's going to happen to her?"

"She'll be charged for the attempted murder of you and first-degree murder of her unborn baby. She'll no doubt be committed to a psychiatric unit for a long time, if she survives. I doubt that she'll ever go to trial, she's in bad shape. The doctors don't have much hope for her recovery. Nate and I are going to have you stay with us, while you recuperate, no arguments. You can't stay, and we'll work out our schedules." Tammy gave her the "don't mess with me" look, and Maggie sighed.

"Let's wait and see what happens. I don't want to think about it right now."

"There are other things that you won't want to think about, like how you made the entertainment gossip news again. *Entertainment Tonight* and *The Insider* both had ten-minute pieces on the shooting in last night's episode. They gave it more coverage than who attended the ball-drop in Times Square, and which bands played live. The tabloids are having a field day too. Reporters are camped out in the media room for updates. We had the hospital put a lid on it for now, but you know we're going to have to give them something so they'll leave."

Maggie sighed again. "Maybe there'll be an explosion in the Middle East and I'll be on the back burner and forgotten."

"And maybe pigs fly," Nate said as he woke up. "They won't forget for a long while. Even if they do, once the movie comes out, they'll drag it all back up again. You're in for a media blitz."

Maggie started to say something, when Dr. Diamond entered the room surrounded by the neurosurgery residents and fellows. "You're awake, good, Maggie, all things considering, you're doing fairly well. How are you feeling?" He smiled down at her, taking her hand in his big one.

"I'm sore, but on a scale of 1-10, only about a 4. And, before you ask, no numbness or tingling anywhere. I'm good to go, so can I?" She grinned saucily at him, knowing that this was usually the first question his patients asked.

He laughed and shook his head. "I'm glad your sense of humor is intact. I think you already know the answer to that. We'll take it one day at a time. Now, the guys will help you roll over, so I can look at your back."

Two of the fellows moved forward, and helped logroll Maggie onto her side, she took a deep breath as they rolled her, but it came out more of a groan as the movement sent pain through her body.

"Dressing looks good, no oozing," He took the surgical dressing off and looked at the incision. "Best closing job I've done since my Plastics rotation. It'll hardly leave a scar; you can wear that backless dress they brought you in with, and there won't be any indication of surgery."

She could hear the smile in his voice since he knew she hardly ever dressed like that.

"You, Rogers, redress this incision, and make sure you don't contaminate it. Dr. Dean will be in to take a look at your leg, that's the more serious injury."

Maggie chuckled and snarked, "Are you sure you wouldn't rather have a nurse redress it? After all, the chief of surgery and his fellows redressing the wound of a mere nurse, think of your image."

Dr. Diamond smilingly shook his head. "Maybe you're right. Can you stay on your side until I get one of them in here?"

She heard him move out the door and slumped against the side rail.

Maggie grasped the side rail in an attempt to keep on her side with her good leg dangling over the bed, but the two Fellows stayed where they were, and held her. She glanced up at them and gave them a smile.

"Thanks, guys, for holding onto me, I'm still a little wobbly."

They both nodded and mumbled something that sounded like "No problem," but she wasn't sure with the commotion in the hall. Sounds of loud voices moved closer to her room. Nate and Tammy opened the door to step out, when David burst into the room.

Chapter 26

"Maggie, oh, my God, Maggie!" he managed to get out, before Nate took him by the arm, and moved him none too gently back into the hall.

David tried to squirm out of his grasp, but Nate was tenacious, and escorted David down the hall to the waiting room.

"Dr. Willis, I don't think Maggie wants to see you. You are aware of what happened to her? Your wife tried to kill her. Did you forget about that, or the fact that your wife is dying?"

David looked up at Nate. "I heard. I found out some time ago that Linda was pregnant with someone else's baby. I told her I wanted a divorce. She told me she would never agree to it. If I pursued it, she would make me sorry. I didn't know she would take it out on Maggie."

Nate nodded. "She thought that you were trying to get Maggie back, she saw you talking to her several times, even if it was only at the hospital. She was not going to let you go, especially to Maggie. She thought Maggie was playing with you by seeing Tyler, to make you jealous."

"Was she behind the incidents that happened on the movie set, too?"

"No, that was unrelated to the phone calls and attacks on Maggie. We have him in custody; he just didn't like that fact that Kate Soffel was being portrayed as a victim in a movie, when she was an active participant in the whole thing."

"I'm glad of that anyway." Nate cocked his head at him. "I mean, I'm glad she wasn't responsible for the movie crew being injured."

David couldn't make eye contact with Nate.

"Is Maggie going to be all right?"

"Eventually, Drs. Diamond and Dean say she has a long road ahead of her. There was a lot of muscle damage to her leg when the bullet shattered her femur. The bullet near her spine was not as problematic. She may not be able to work in the E.D. again. That would be worse than death for her, I think."

David looked away from Nate. "Do you need me for anything else, I'd like to see for myself that Maggie is okay." He started to rise, but Nate pushed him back into the chair.

"I don't think you understand. Maggie does not want to see you. If you persist in attempting to see her, I will restrain you, with arrest if need be." Nate's tone was grim.

David sat silent for a moment, then nodded. He stood slowly, and walked in the opposite direction. Nate returned to Maggie's room, by now, the dressing had been replaced, and she was once again comfortably resting. She smiled when she saw Nate enter the room.

"Did you send David on his way?"

"Yes, I told him you didn't want to see him, and if he attempted again, I'd arrest him. He left quietly." Nate took his seat again as his cell phone rang. He looked at the caller ID and handed the phone to Maggie. "Do you want to talk to him?"

Maggie's expression was puzzled as she took the phone and looked at the ID. She nodded, and held the phone to her ear.

"Tyler?"

"Maggie, I was so worried! I heard about it on my flight here. On board news had the whole story, they made is sound as if you had died. Nate told me you were out of danger, that you had been in surgery, and that it was not life threatening. May I come to see you? I have a lot to explain and it should be done in person, as I told you earlier." His voice was calm, but Maggie could hear the slight quaver, that gave away the fact that he wasn't as sure of himself as he let on. She wanted to see him and looked up at Nate and Tammy who both nodded.

"I'd like that, Ty. I'm not going anywhere." She handed the phone back to Nate, and slid back against the pillows, closing her eyes. She sighed and opened one eye to look at Tammy. "You really think I should let him explain? He went back to Hollywood and forgot about me, just like I thought he would."

Tammy sat on the edge of her bed and took her hand, looking at Nate for confirmation. He nodded to her and moved his chair closer to Maggie's bed. "I may be speaking out of turn here, but Tyler didn't forget you while he was in California. He called me every day to see how you were. He thought if he left you'd be safe."

"What! What are you talking about? He went for the premiere of his movie and stayed to be with Heidi!" Tammy was shaking her head, then winced as the room spun with the movement.

"Yes, he had to go for the premiere, but he stayed and was seen out with Heidi for you, well partly. He wanted to make sure that if he *was* the reason behind the phone calls, then you wouldn't get any more if he was out of the picture. He also was doing a favor for Heidi, so that she would be able to land the series she was up for by acting as her boyfriend."

Maggie stared at her wide-eyed and open-mouthed.

"Honey, close your mouth. You were his main concern. He called every day; he really missed spending Christmas with you. He wanted to surprise you by being here for New Year's Eve, but his flight was delayed in Chicago, due to weather and then he heard what happened. It was all we could do to keep him calm until he landed here. He came right to the hospital, but we convinced him to wait until you woke up, and we could see if you were strong enough to deal with him."

CHAPTER 27

Nate and Tammy left to check on Taser, and to get dinner. Tyler arrived about an hour later, carrying a bouquet of Spider mums and a vase. He stood in the doorway to Maggie's room looking at her, scarcely breathing. She was lying there with her eyes closed, face too pale, but relaxed. He was hesitant to wake her, so he moved quietly to the chair that Nate had vacated earlier. Ty placed the vase on the stand next to her bed and drank her in, his heart overflowed with love for her, and he was struck with how alone he felt when he had been in California, without her. The hollow feeling was worse when he heard what had happened at her house on New Year's Eve, he almost lost her, and despite Nate's assurances that she would be all right, he knew he had to see for himself. Now, looking at her sleeping, he felt whole again.

Maggie opened her eyes and looked into Ty's bright blue ones. "How long have you been here? Why didn't you wake me?"

"Only a little while, I wanted you to rest. I was so afraid that I had lost you. Maggie, I was never with Heidi, not like that anyway. She's an old friend, and we were helping each other through a difficult time. I thought that if I...."

Maggie placed a finger on his lips to silence him. "I know. Tammy told me all about it this afternoon. I don't understand why you let me think that you forgot about me, or didn't want me anymore. That hurt so much. Why didn't you just tell me you were going to stay in California a while to stop the phone calls? I would have understood."

Ty shook his head. "Maggie, unless you thought I was gone for good, you wouldn't have been convincing. You can't lie, and no one who knew you would believe I was cheating on you, if you knew the truth. I'm really sorry I put you through that." He took her hands in his. "Can you forgive me?"

Maggie looked into his eyes trying to find the answer to his question; they were clear and bright, with no trace of deceit. She leaned her head toward his, kissed him tenderly, and felt tears threatening to overflow. She nodded, and buried her head in his neck. He felt the dampness on his skin, and lifted her head. He wiped the tears away with his thumbs and kissed her. gently at first, then with desire.

"Thank you," he whispered against her lips.

She pulled back, moaning but not with desire. "I need to lie back," she sighed, and moved to get in a more comfortable position, pulling him with her. "Will you stay 'til I fall asleep?"

"I'll stay as long as you want me to." He curled next to her, and pulled her into his embrace.

She fell asleep with his arms wrapped around her; he stayed watching her sleep, his spirit lighter than it had been since Thanksgiving. After a while, he too fell into a deep, dreamless sleep.

Maggie dreamt she was sitting by a roaring fire that was slowly burning her skin. She tried to move back, but was stopped by a vise getting tighter by the moment. She struggled, and suddenly woke to find herself enveloped in Ty's arms. She realized why she was so hot; it was like sleeping with a furnace with him. She gazed up at his face, slack in repose, and marveled at how beautiful he was; she never really got the opportunity to study him when he slept. If his face was interesting with animation, it was even more so while he relaxed. She moved closer to his face, and dropped a kiss at the corner of his mouth, then moved to the other side, finally ending the kiss on the center of his lips. She nibbled his bottom lip until he began to stir, and his eyes opened, glowing midnight blue, as he regarded her.

"Honey, I think you'd better stop that, you aren't in any shape for this to go farther, and I am beginning to lose control."

She blushed, and started to sidle away, but he caught her and pulled her in for a deep, erotic kiss. Her blush deepened as the door to her room opened, and Becky, the night nurse, entered smiling. Maggie succeeded in pulling out of Ty's arms, wiggling to the opposite side rail.

"I'm just going to check your vitals, and then I'll leave you alone. I might suggest that I wake you before the day shift comes on, so you won't be caught." Maggie groaned and Tyler laughed.

"Thanks, I'd appreciate that. Not that anything is going on, Maggie's too fragile, but I just need to be close to her."

It was Becky's turn to blush and she nodded as she picked up the blood pressure cuff and proceeded to assess Maggie's vital signs. She grinned at Maggie and wished them both a goodnight, closing the door again as she left. Maggie groaned again and mumbled against Ty's chest.

"What was that? I didn't hear you." Ty brushed his lips against Maggie's hair.

"I'll never be able to show my face around here again," she muttered.

"Why, just because you have a hot guy in bed with you and the staff found out?" Ty smirked at her, and she giggled, suddenly not caring that the whole hospital would know that Ty was in her bed.

Ty helped her turn over, careful of the hardware jutting out of her left leg, and spooned against her, stroking her hair, her shoulder, down her arm, to her hip and leg. He repeated the motion until he heard her steady breathing, and knew she'd fallen asleep again.

Ty didn't go back to sleep, his mind wouldn't stop replaying the events of New Year's Eve. He was stuck in Chicago, waiting for the blizzard to end so he could get to Maggie. When the news broadcast said that Maggie had been shot, by a crazed stalker, and was in critical condition, he tried every connection he could to get a flight out of Chicago. It was only when his cell phone vibrated, and Nate called, that he finally calmed enough to not be arrested for domestic terrorism. He frowned at the thought—that she could have died, and he would never see her face, or feel or lips on his again. He pulled Maggie closer to him, causing her to whimper softly in her sleep, he backed off and contented himself with simply holding her. He found himself dozing, but woke with every movement and sound from Maggie. He knew that she would need care and therapy after her release from the hospital, he started putting a plan together. With his mind finally resolved, he slept.

Becky knocked and entered the room, to find Tyler already out of Maggie's bed and sitting in the chair next to it. "Good morning," she whispered. "How did she sleep?"

"Better than I did. I couldn't get my brain to shut down, I kept thinking about how I almost lost her."

Becky nodded. "She was very lucky. She's not going to be very happy about months of physical therapy, though. That leg is pretty messed up." Becky grimaced, and walked toward the bed. "Maggie," she touched Maggie's arm. "Maggie, I need to get your vitals for morning rounds. I can help you get washed up if you like, too. I waited to come in here last so that you two could have more time together."

Maggie extended her arm to Becky who quickly measured her blood pressure. She listened to her breathing and heart, then asked if she was having any pain. Maggie shook her head, "I used the machine right before you came in, it's okay for now. Do I get breakfast today? I'm starving." Becky smiled ruefully, and shook her head no.

"Not real food, full liquids. If you do okay, I'm sure you'll get food for lunch."

She handed Maggie a toothbrush and toothpaste, along with a cup of water and a basin to spit the toothpaste and rinse water out. While Maggie brushed her teeth, Becky filled a basin with warm water and brought it back to the bedside stand. Both women looked at Ty, who shrugged and said he'd go get some coffee, and allow the women to take care of things. Becky sighed as Tyler left the room. Once the door closed behind him both Becky and Maggie began to giggle.

"He has one fine ass." Becky smirked. "You are a lucky, lucky woman."

Maggie nodded. "I agree about his ass, and yes, I'd have to say that I am lucky to have him in my life." She looked thoughtful and added, "At least for now."

Becky looked askance at her and asked what she meant.

"Isn't it obvious? He isn't going to want to wait around for me to get back on my feet. Even if he does, I don't know how mobile I'll be. What if I can't work anymore? I don't want people to think I'm with him because he'll take care of me. And I certainly don't want him to stick around because he feels sorry for me."

"I don't think that's the case. You didn't see him when he got here. Nate and Tammy told me that they had to calm him down before he caused a major scene in Chicago because he couldn't get a flight out. He was frantic. He just told me that he couldn't sleep last night, in spite of holding you, because he almost lost you. That doesn't sound like someone who feels sorry for you; it sounds like someone who loves you."

Becky continued to wash Maggie, as much as she could with the bandages, allowing Maggie to wash her face and chest. Maggie's eyes sought Becky's and saw that the other woman was telling the truth.

"I love him, too, so much. I thought he didn't want me anymore when he went to California. I just wanted to die. When Linda shot me, and I thought it was too late, that's when the thought of never seeing him again was too much, that's when I knew I loved him. He called on Christmas Day to ask if I would see him when he got back to Pittsburgh after New Year's. I wouldn't answer him then, but as the blackness swept around me, I knew that if he asked again, I'd say yes." Tears welled in her eyes, but she blinked them away.

Becky changed the subject. "Do you want me to pull your hair back in a braid? It won't get so tangled that way."

Maggie smiled gratefully at her and nodded. Becky brushed her hair, working the tangles out, and eventually had it smooth. She brushed it up and back, and began braiding it.

"Your hair is so soft and thick. How long have you had it long like this?"

"Forever, it seems like. I get it trimmed to keep it straight and neat, but never had it cut short. I'm too lazy to bother with styling it. This way I can pull it back or up, and I'm good to go."

"That must be nice, I have to blow mine dry and straighten it, or it's a mass of frizz." Becky laughed and finished the braid. "There, all done. I'm off tonight, but I'll be daylight tomorrow. See you then," and she was out the door.

The hospital began the bustle of the morning routine: shift change and new nurses on duty, housekeeping moping the floors, and the doctors coming in and seemingly pleased with her progress. She begged for real food for lunch and they agreed. They asked about her pain and how much pain medication she was using. She answered that the pain wasn't that bad unless she was moving, especially her leg and that she disliked the feeling the narcotics gave her. Dr. Dean changed the medication to something less strong, but warned her that he would go back to the narcotics if he felt it was necessary. He also said that they would get her out of bed later in the morning. As they left, Dr. Diamond and his entourage entered, the two doctors conferred for a few minutes, and the orthopedic team continued out the door.

"Well, I hear that you're to get real food for lunch, and you're to get out of bed later today. How are you feeling, really Maggie, I've known you for years, and I know how you are."

"I'm okay, really. My leg hurts, but it's less than it was yesterday. My back itches more than hurts. It's my stomach I'm worried about, it thinks my throat has been hacked since it's not getting any food! I can't wait until lunch."

Dr. Diamond examined her face and sat on the edge of the bed. "Now, tell me what's really bothering you."

Maggie sighed. "You know me too well, I can't hide anything from you, can I? I'm worried about how long this will take to heal. You know that we only get twelve weeks sick leave, what if I'm not ready to come back after that? Dr. Dean told me it could take months for my leg to heal and get strength back, and that's only if I'm fortunate enough to get adequate strength back. What will I do if I can't come back to the E.D.?"

Dr. Diamond took her hand in his. "Maggie, I learned a long time ago not to borrow trouble. You know what I say, 'When God closes a door, he always opens a window.' Just take each day as it comes, and work toward your goal. Things have a habit of working out the way they are meant to be." He squeezed her hand and said, "If worse comes to worst, you could always work for me, get your Nurse Practitioner Certification, you've talked about it often enough. If you don't want to work for me, think about the transplant service, they're always looking for someone with your background to talk to families, about donating their loved one's organs. You assist with that now, and you're good at it. You will have a lot of opportunities once you get back on your feet. For now, just concentrate on getting out of here, and getting better." Dr. Diamond patted her hand and got up to leave.

Maggie held his hand and squeezed it. "I appreciate the pep talk, I wasn't thinking past my nose. You're right, I can use the time to think about my options and make a decision when I'm given the okay to go back to work. I'll be fine in the meantime. Maybe, I can even start some online classes for an advanced degree. You've given me something to think about, thank you." Maggie squeezed his hand.

"My pleasure, my dear; I can't think of anyone here who would want to lose you." With that, he left the room.

Maggie sank back into the bed, cursing the uncomfortable mattress, and wondered how patients tolerated it. She also wondered where Ty was, he'd been gone for a long time. As if he read her thoughts, the door opened, and he walked in with an attractive older woman who had his bright blue eyes and drop-dead gorgeous smile.

CHAPTER 28

Tyler walked over to Maggie's bed, leaned in to kiss her deeply, and said, "I want you to meet my mother." He reached his arm back to the woman hovering by the door.

She moved toward the bed and Ty took her hand.

"Mom, this is my Maggie."

Maggie gaped, "*His* Maggie," when did that happen? She glanced up at Ty then to his mother, then back again to Tyler.

He thought she looked nervous, hadn't he told her he was bringing his mother to meet her? His mind searched his actions from this morning when Becky had arrived, and remembered that he had only thought about how his mom could help, but never said anything to Maggie. *Oh, hell, I didn't tell her, no wonder she looks uneasy, this isn't the way she would want to meet my family.* "I'm sorry, sweetheart, I meant to tell you that she was coming to visit after the holidays, but I forgot to."

He looked so contrite, so Maggie didn't say what she would have, if they'd been alone.

"It's very nice to meet you, Mrs. Sinclair."

Maggie held out her hand to the woman, who ignored it, and instead, leaned in and hugged her as best she could, with the side rails and the newly installed trapeze, to help Maggie move, in the bed.

"It's I who am glad to meet you, Ty's talked of nothing but you since you met. If you ask me, the boy is smitten." Tyler had the grace to flush, but wisely kept his mouth closed. "I've been looking forward to meeting you, but this isn't how I imagined it, you injured and in the hospital. As soon as you're out of here, we'll get you comfortable, and make sure you have everything you need." Maggie stared at her then at Ty.

"I'm sorry, what did you say?"

"Don't tell me Ty didn't tell you about this, either!" She turned to her son, and shook her head. "Really, son, what were you thinking? You can't just spring this on her."

Once again, he flushed, and tried to defend himself, but Mrs. Sinclair was having none of it.

She turned to Maggie. "Tyler seems to think that you won't be able to stay alone, and can't bear the thought of sending you to a rehab facility, until you're able to get around and take care of yourself. He's going to take you home, and I'm going to stay with you while you do your therapy. Since he didn't see fit to ask your opinion, I'm asking. Do you want to go to his house and have me babysit you?"

Maggie didn't know what to say, the thought of going to Ty's home was something she had wished for, but not necessarily with his mother in tow, and what about Taser? "Mrs. Sinclair," she began, but the older woman cut her off.

"None of this 'Mrs. Sinclair nonsense,' I'm Joanna."

Once again, Maggie found her hand engulfed in the older woman's.

"Joanna, I don't know what to say, this seems like a terrible inconvenience, having you stuck with me, for who knows how long. Besides, I have a rather large dog, I would miss him terribly, not to mention how he would miss me."

Ty interrupted, "That's not a problem. I have plenty of room for him to run; of course he would come with you. Mom's used to our assorted menagerie, so one more dog won't matter." He tried to woo her with his sad gaze, but Maggie was having none of that.

"Since I'm not ready to be discharged yet, it's a moot point. I will think about it however, and will let you know."

Tyler wisely dropped the subject, and they began to talk about other things, including wrapping up filming for the movie. The remaining scenes would be done in the sound stage, rerecording the dialogue that was muffled, due to outside noises, when the original scene was shot. Ty would be going back to California soon, for about two weeks, then would be back. In the meantime, he told her, Joanna would be staying at Maggie's and looking after Taser, if that was okay with her. Maggie could only shake her head, and say that if Joanna had no problem with it, then neither did she.

Ty kissed her goodbye, and told her to get some rest, while he took his mom to Maggie's house and introduced her to Taser, Nate, and Tammy. He'd be back soon, and would bring her something to eat, since she was once again complaining that she was hungry. Maggie took his advice and dozed, until the physical therapist came in to start working with her. Jason helped her use the trapeze to get out of bed and into a wheel chair. Once she accomplished that, he pushed the chair into the bathroom, and helped her get onto the commode. Maggie exhaled and smiled up at him.

"This is so good. I hate bedpans. This means I can get washed at the sink instead of using that basin. Let me try this a few more times, so I can do it without help."

Jason and Maggie worked getting from the bed to the wheel chair, and then to the commode and back again. After an hour of steady moving, Maggie admitted that she was tired. Jason helped get her situated in the bed, and said he'd be back tomorrow. Maggie fell asleep almost before Jason left the room.

That's how Ty found her when he returned, carrying a bag from China Palace filled with all of Maggie's favorites. The odors wafting from the bag effectively awakened her, and she sat up trying to grab the bag from Tyler's grasp.

"Not so fast, let me set it up for you. I have everything that you have circled on your take out menu at home."

He began to take containers out of the bags, and set them on the overbed table. He wasn't kidding when he said he got all of her favorites: General Tso's Chicken, Kung Po Chicken, Sweet & Sour Shrimp, vegetable Lo Mein, Crab Rangoon, beef fried rice, steamed rice, Hot & Sour soup, and egg rolls with duck sauce.

She gaped at him in amazement. "Who is going to eat all of this?" she squealed with delight, grabbing the chopsticks and a container of vegetable Lo Mein.

Ty just grinned at her, delighted to see animation return to her face. She pulled Lo Mein out of the container shoving it into her mouth, when she realized what she was doing. She flushed, setting the container back on the table.

"Would you dish some of everything out for me so I don't act like a starved refugee?"

"Of course, tell me when to stop dishing." He picked up a plate, and began to spoon the food from the containers, until her plate was heaping with a hearty portion of each. He handed the plate to her pretending to count his fingers, as she took it from him.

She giggled at his silliness, and watched as he helped himself to the food. Only when he had filled his plate, and sat down, did she begin to eat. For the next several minutes, the only sound was lips smacking and moans of pleasure, as Maggie all but inhaled the contents of her plate. When she finished, she looked up to find Tyler staring at her grinning. She looked down at her plate and flushed.

"I guess I was a little hungry," she said, embarrassed and red-faced.

"Do you want more? There's some of everything left." He picked up the containers and handed them off to her.

She shook her head. "I had enough, thank you," she said sheepishly. "You must think I'm a pig."

"I've seen you eat before, I know you have a healthy appetite, and you also haven't eaten real food since New Year's Eve. I'm glad to see that you're eating. Now that I've softened you up, maybe we should talk about you moving into my house when you're discharged."

"Is that why you brought all my favorites, to get me to go to L.A. with you? That's pretty sneaky." Maggie smiled sadly up at him. "I'm not sure that's a good idea. I'll have appointments with doctors here. My friends are here, my house, Taser…." She trailed off when Tyler took her hand.

"Maggie, I'm sure your doctors can refer you to ones in L.A. Taser can come with us. Nate and Tammy will watch your house. I don't want you alone. My mom can be with you all day."

Maggie shook her head at him. "Ty, I love that you want to help. I trust the docs I have; I don't like having to meet new ones, and having them get me back to normal. I also don't like being dependent on anyone, I'm not used to it. Please understand that."

Ty took a deep breath before speaking again. "Baby, I love you. I know you don't believe that, especially after what happened after Thanksgiving. I thought I was doing the right thing, by protecting you. Would you let me stay here with you then? My mom doesn't have to be back in New York for a while. Let us both stay, please. I can drive you wherever you need to go."

"And what happens when you get a call for a new movie, or to do the publicity for this one? This recovery is going to take months. My leg is a mess, and unlike in the movies, I'm not going to be on my feet next week. You don't know what you're getting into." She tried to keep from whining as her frustration with him.

He wrapped her in his arms. "I know exactly how long this will take. I don't want you to have to do it by yourself. Please, Maggie, let my mom and me move in with you."

Maggie didn't have a chance to respond, because David knocked and entered the room. "May I come in?" he asked hesitantly, but continued to move into the room.

Tyler made a growling sound deep in his chest as he turned to look at the other man. He was about to answer him when Maggie spoke.

"Yes."

David gave a sideways glance at Tyler as he moved toward Maggie. "I know I'm the last person you want to talk to, but I'd like to clear the air. I should have been honest with you when I started seeing Linda...." His voice trailed off, he looked embarrassed and ashamed.

Maggie didn't say anything, waiting for him to continue. Ty looked at him with contempt, and sat down in the chair next to Maggie.

"Linda made me feel important; she chased me, even knowing I was seeing you. You know things weren't all that great between us, that was my fault, I rushed you instead of taking my time with you, and enjoying the two of us together. Then, when she told me she was pregnant, I should have talked to you, instead of avoiding you. I was feeling guilty about the whole mess. Then you left the O.R. and transferred to the E.D. That made me feel even worse, because I knew how the transplant surgeons felt about you; they were ready to string me up by the short hairs." David took a deep breath, as if waiting for Maggie to say something, she only examined him as if she were assessing a patient who wasn't telling her the whole story, so he continued somewhat reluctantly. "Linda had an amniocentesis right around Halloween. She tried to hide it from me but I saw the results and I knew I couldn't be the father. When I confronted her, she laughed and said it was true. There were so many candidates for that title, she said that she wasn't sure who the father was; I felt even more of a fool, for falling for her crap. I realized, then, that her interest in me was her way of getting back at you for your promotion to Transplant Surgical Coordinator. She had been sure she was getting that position, and then dating the hot, new, neurosurgeon, her words not mine by the way, would put you in your place. She went on and on about how you own that gorgeous house and the lodge and how the surgeons fawn over you." He tried to smile at her, but it looked more like a grimace. "I know you don't owe me anything, but I want to ask your forgiveness for how I treated you."

David held his hand out to Maggie and, after a slight hesitation, she took it.

"I forgave you some time ago. I don't think we'll ever be able to get past this, but I don't hate you anymore."

David raised her hand to his cheek, "Thank you. Now, I'll leave you to rest."

He released Maggie's hand and walked out of her room head held high. He hesitated at the door, but then continued without looking back. Tears were streaming down her face, unnoticed, until Ty took her face in his hands and wiped them away with his thumbs. His eyes met her tear-filled ones, he moved closer to wrap his arms around her. She cried softly into the hollow of his shoulder, as he rubbed her back. After the tears were done, she shuddered, and drew back to look at him. He wiped her face gently and leaned in to kiss her softly.

"Do you still love him?" Ty's voice was steady, but Maggie could hear the agony behind his words.

"No, I was hurt that he could just ignore me like he did when I found him with Linda. As time passed, I realized it was anger and embarrassment and betrayal more than love that I felt. I heard from all my friends how it felt to be dumped by someone, how devastated they were afterwards. Almost as if they had no reason to live. I felt none of that. I had been working those thoughts out when I drove up to the lodge to close it for the winter. That day I was cleaning in the attic loft, I sat and thought about my strong reaction to you, and how that could be, if I were still in love with David."

Tyler wrapped his arms around her, and kissed her gently, at first, then with insistence for her to open to him. She moaned and leaned closer to him, her tongue dancing with his until Maggie had to stop him.

"I can't breathe," she laughed up at him.

He kissed her forehead and got up from the bed to sit demurely in the chair again.

"Let me take care of you for now. Since you won't come to L.A., at least let my Mom stay with you, just to get you to your appointments and help you manage."

Maggie nodded after a few tense seconds, agreeing.

"Good. God, Maggie when I thought you'd died, part of me did, too. I love you; you must know that. I want to marry you."

Maggie looked askance at him, her mouth gaping open and her eyes huge. "What did you say?" She barely whispered the words.

"You heard me, I want to marry you. This isn't an official proposal, I have a plan for that, but I wanted you to know my intentions. When you're back on your feet, we have plans to make."

Maggie wasn't sure what to say, she was too dumbfounded to speak anyway. She could only gaze at him.

Tyler leaned toward her again and kissed her. "I have a lot to do to get your house ready for you, and my mom moved in. I'll be back tonight. I love you."

Maggie nodded that she heard him but was still speechless.

CHAPTER 29

T he next few days were a blur of physical therapy, and preparations for leaving the hospital. Tyler and Joanna were there every day to watch her progress, and to learn how to care for the fixator attached to her leg. After eighteen days, Maggie was finally released, and she couldn't wait to get into her own bed. She really wanted a shower, and had a plan to do it, as soon as she got home, with Joanna's help. Tyler picked her up in her truck so she could stretch her leg out on the back seat.

When she walked in the house, the first thing she noticed was that the Christmas decorations had been packed away, and the house was spotless. She turned, shook her head, and pointed to Ty.

"I didn't want you to come back to the mess that Linda made, and I didn't think you'd be in any shape to put the ornaments away. I was very careful with them. I wiped each one with a damp cloth and wrapped them in the fabric and plastic you had for them," he said as she continued to look around the room.

"Thank you. You were right I really couldn't face doing that myself." She leaned up to kiss him, then turned slowly to go into the kitchen. "Where's Taser?"

"He's with Nate and Tammy, we thought we'd leave him there until you got settled and in a sitting position, before he came bounding in and knocking you over. Once you get comfortable, I'll go up and get him."

Maggie nodded and sat at the table. She looked around her kitchen and sighed. "I'd like to sit a minute, then wrap my leg in one of the big yard bags so I can shower."

Joanna patted her shoulder, and went out the back door. She came back a few minutes later with one of the large green leaf bags. She and Maggie made their way up the stairs to Maggie's room. Once there, Joanna helped Maggie undo the sweat pants. Joanna had cut the seams open, and added strips of hook-and-loop strips to the fabric, so that the leg of the sweats would go over the fixator. Maggie got into the shower stall, with Joanna helping to get the leaf bag over her leg and secure it to keep the wound dry. Maggie turned the shower on, and luxuriated under the hot spray. She sat on the bench soaping her hair and body. She relaxed under the hand held spray sighing deeply. Bed baths just didn't cut it. When the water began to cool, Maggie reluctantly turned off the shower, and opened the door to reach for the towel warmer, only to encounter a warm masculine hand.

"I timed that just right. Let me dry you, I don't want you to fall with that slippery bag on your leg."

Tyler stepped into the shower stall, wrapped a towel around her wet hair, and with another warmed towel, began to pat her dry. He removed the leaf bag from her leg before allowing her to stand up, but instead of allowing her to walk into her bedroom, he swept her up and carried her, depositing her on the bed. He grabbed another altered pair of sweats, and helped her into them. Maggie finished dressing, and the two of them made their way downstairs to the living room. Tyler left to get Taser, who did indeed come bounding into the house, and promptly put his paws on Maggie's good leg trying to lick her face. She rubbed his ears and buried her face in his soft fur, tears burning her eyes.

Taser never left her side for the remainder of the evening, not wanting to leave even to eat. They all followed Taser into the kitchen and had dinner together. The evening passed quickly after that, and Maggie tried to stifle a yawn. Joanna caught it, and suggested that she go up to bed. Maggie reluctantly went to her room, with Tyler coming in right behind her.

"Hey, you don't have to come to bed yet, it's early. I'm just beat."

Tyler said nothing, he just helped her undress and tucked her into her bed.

"Ohhhhhhhh, this feels so good, I missed my bed."

Tyler bent to kiss her goodnight. "I'll be up in a while. Go to sleep, baby." He pulled the quilt up around her and turned to leave.

Taser came in and plopped down at the foot of the bed. Maggie snuggled into the bed and soon fell asleep.

Tyler had managed to convince Jason and his wife to come to the house to do her therapy sessions, since Maggie worked better when they were overseeing the sessions. They would take turns coming after work on the days she didn't go in for therapy. This meant that Maggie had therapy every day to strengthen her leg. She couldn't wait to get the fixator off and start to bear weight on it.

By the end of February, the fixator came off and Maggie began the second phase of her rehab, using crutches instead of a walker. She would begin to put weight on her leg as she walked. The crutches made her clumsy, but she was just happy to have the fixator removed. Joanna returned to her home in New York, but made Maggie promise to call if she needed anything. She and Tyler flew to his home in L.A. for two weeks while he met with Mike to talk about a new movie, and prepare to promote *The Warden's Wife*. Maggie used his pool and swam laps or did water aerobics, to strengthen her leg muscles. She was beginning to feel herself and started thinking about going back to work. Her conversation with Drs. Sebastian and Diamond had started her reflecting on what direction she wanted her career to go. She loved being a nurse, but knew that because of her injury, she wouldn't be able to continue the pace of staff nursing. The idea of becoming a nurse practitioner and working with the transplant team was appealing. Each afternoon she would research various programs. Since she wanted to focus on transplantation, she would have to find a program that would allow her to complete a practicum in that field. She wanted to keep occupied while Ty was off doing the promotion tour. Once she found a program, she spoke to the admissions department and the nursing department, she sat down with Ty and told him of her decision. His initial reaction was one of surprise.

"I thought you could travel with me. I wanted to show you what your life with me would be like. I didn't consider you going back to school." He couldn't keep the surprise or hurt from his voice.

"Ty, my going to school won't stop me from traveling with you. My classes will be online, at least until I start my practicum, and that won't be until my course work is completed. This will give me something to do while you're with the media. I realize I won't be able to work the way I did in the past, but I don't want to just sit and do nothing."

Tyler looked thoughtful, then nodded. "You're right as usual. I can't see you not being busy. I heard what Dr. Sebastian said about your skills with families and the transplant team. It's where you belong. So tell me about this program."

They spent the next several hours talking about the program. The next term would begin in August, so she had the rest of the spring and summer to travel with him, and enjoy the summer, working on her strength training and leg exercises. Maggie was much happier now that she had a direction.

Maggie returned home without Tyler for a few days. She was planning to meet him in New York to meet the rest of his family. She thought that she should be nervous about this, but because of her weeks with Joanna, she was merely looking forward to meeting his brother and sisters. She had spoken to them on the phone at various times during Joanna's stay with her, and they seemed to be welcoming, and just a little bit incredulous that Tyler was finally going to settle down. Maggie wasn't sure about that, after her first night home from the hospital, nothing else had been said about marriage.

The day before she was to leave for New York, Tammy called her. "I wanted you to hear this from me and not the news, and to prepare you for a media onslaught again. Linda died this morning. She never regained consciousness. The hospital tried to suppress the information but someone on the staff leaked it. There'll be a uniformed officer at your door within the hour, and I'll take you to the airport in the morning. I think this news may bring the media down on you to rehash what happened on New Year's."

"I can't say that I'm sorry she's dead, even if she was my friend at one time. She caused too much damage to too many people. Thanks for the heads-up."

Maggie hung up the phone and called Tyler to let him know. She didn't want him to hear it on the news either and be worried about her. After an all too short conversation, she went up to her room to pack for tomorrow.

Tyler's family welcomed Maggie with opened arms. She was made to feel at home and comfortable. After dinner, Tyler took her for a walk in the large garden, enjoying the evening and the sunset. "I like your family," she said as they sat on a bench under a large elm tree.

"They like you as well. They are surprised that I've brought a girl home, you're a first for them. They aren't sure what to make of you." Tyler took her hand in his and brought it to his lips. "Maggie, I love you, I fell in love with you at the lodge, and it's only become deeper since then." He slid off the bench onto one knee, and pulled a small box from his pocket. "Will you marry me?" He opened the box to a beautiful pear-shaped diamond set in gold with inset diamonds along the band.

Maggie felt tears streaming down her face, as she nodded to him and whispered, "Yes." Tyler took her hand in his and slipped the ring on her finger.

EPILOGUE

In the months that followed Maggie continued with her physical therapy and although she was walking, it wasn't without difficulty or help. She hated the walker and as long as she needed to use it she couldn't go back to work. The pain and limp were most noticeable when she was fatigued. She began an online program to obtain her Nurse Practitioner degree and kept busy with her studies when Ty was away filming. She often found herself looking at the sparkling diamond on her left hand wondering at the miracle that brought Tyler into her life. She wondered what would have happened if she hadn't listened to Taser that wintery October day.

One event darkened the overall pleasure of Maggie's world happened one bright May morning. Dan Diamond arrived at her door looking grim. Maggie backed away from the door and watched him as he slowly entered the living room.

"Dan, what's wrong?"

Dan took a deep breath and sank into the camelback sofa. "Sit down, Maggie." His eyes were filled with anguish and discomfort.

Maggie sat next to him and he took her hands in his.

"David's dead. He didn't show for his morning surgery and didn't answer his phone. Marc Dean sent the police to his house. He hanged himself. We, the police and I, thought it might be easier to hear it from me than have the police tell you." He pulled a small blue envelope from his pocket and handed it to her. "He left this for you."

Numbly, Maggie took the envelope and opened it.

Maggie,

No words can say how sorry I am about how I treated you; I know you said you forgave me but I can't forgive myself. They say Karma's a bitch and they're right. I got what I deserved with Linda, but you didn't deserve any of it. You have no idea how loved you are by the hospital staff, housekeeping to surgeons all love you and are not at all hesitant in letting me know what they think of me. Not overtly but in little ways. I'm not asking for pity only that I realize what I did. I thought of moving away but no matter where I go people will know who I am and what I did. I'll never be able to shake it off. Tyler's a good man, I've seen how he looks when he's asked about you in interviews. Although he hasn't said so, I know he will be asking to marry you if he hasn't already. Know that I realized too late what you truly meant to me.

David

Maggie handed the missive to Dan while tears ran down her face. Dan read the short note and held his arms open to Maggie who moved into them and cried for the man she had once thought she loved. It was true that much of the misery stemmed from Linda but David was to blame as well for being weak and gullible.

For Tyler's part, he phoned every day either before or after filming. He would have preferred that Maggie travel with him but realized it would hinder her recovery if she had to find new physical therapists every few months. He was proud of her and wanted her to complete her education but he was also selfish enough to want her with him as well. A small part of him was troubled that she might change her mind and decide she didn't want to share his life under the watchful eyes of the paparazzi. These thoughts were quickly banished when they spoke and she regaled him with the wedding plans she was working on with his mother and Tammy. While the tabloids continued to speculate on their relationship, Maggie and Tyler kept the engagement to themselves and family for now. They discussed when to let the media know and Michael was straining any small amount of patience he possessed to break the news. In the end, Michael wasn't the one to break the news. Maggie accompanied Tyler to the red carpet premiere of *The Warden's Wife*, where he lifted Maggie's left hand to show to the paparazzi. The flurry of camera flashes was blinding and the barrage of questions was a cacophony around them.

"When did you propose?"

"When's the wedding?"

"Maggie, are you moving to L.A.?"

"Tyler, does this mean you're retiring?"

The questions followed them into the theatre where Michael was waiting for them with a scowl on his face. "I don't suppose you thought of how this will overshadow the movie, did you?"

Tyler grinned. "No, I think it will add to it since we met while I was making the movie. Aren't you the one who says any publicity is good publicity? This is really good publicity for the movie and serves the added purpose of ending speculation about us." Tyler grinned at him while Michael just shook his head and moved into the seating area.

They kept the details of the wedding to themselves, however, which wasn't difficult, since Maggie could fly under the paparazzi radar while in Pittsburgh. Since the ceremony would be in her hometown, and Maggie had been able to keep it simple and relatively quiet, the media didn't catch wind of it until it was over, and that was only because Michael sent out a press release.

Tammy was the only attendant and Tyler's brother was the best man. Nate gave Maggie away, and had a few "fatherly" words with Tyler, about taking care of her, causing both men to chuckle. The guests consisted of a few close friends from the hospital and Tyler's family. Mike, Heidi, and her partner Katie, were the only show business people in attendance.

Nate's supporting arm allowed Maggie to walk slowly down the aisle toward the altar; she refused to use a cane for the ceremony. Her dress was simple and vintage. The bodice was form-fitting ivory lace with a sweetheart neckline barely hinting at cleavage. The skirt of ivory silk with lace trim billowed out from the fitted waist to form a short train. She wore no veil over her elaborately braided hair, which was held in place with an ivory comb that had belonged to her great-grandmother. Her flowers were white spider mums and peach day lilies. She looked toward the alter to Tyler, who looked every inch the movie star in his black tuxedo. His smile, as she approached him, lit up his face, and made her heart flutter with anticipation. Finally, they stood together in front of the priest and began the traditional wedding vows. When the priest said the words, "You may kiss the bride," Maggie all but threw herself at him and flung her arms around his neck. The kiss lasted for several minutes, until a discreet cough reminded them of where they were. Maggie blushed and slowly pulled away from Tyler; together, they turned and walked back up the aisle Tyler supporting his new wife and holding her hand to start their life.

"The Biddles and Mrs. Soffel Shot and Captured." *The Reading Eagle*. February 1, 1902

CPSIA information can be obtained
at www.ICGtesting.com
Printed in the USA
LVOW07s0046181017
552831LV00023B/891/P

9 781480 937420